# The Adventures of

# Sedgewick Harris

## AF OCONNOR

FOR VERA

# CONTENTS

# ACKNOWLEDGMENTS

Declan Bailey Book Cover / Marketing

Bridget McAuliffe Red Hen Publishing Listowel Co Kerry

Ferdia Mac Anna Producer/Director/Filmmaker

## Preface

Following my retirement from business in 2006 I began writing. These four stories are the first of a series to be published. The inspiration came from my love of Sherlock Holmes and it became my ambition to create a similar character, based in the west of Ireland.

On a whim, I chose Sedgewick Harris to be my private investigator. Along the way the characters of Jonathan, the Major and Inspector Hennessy have been developed and of course the lovely Helen Mannion. It has been a wonderful experience for me to create and follow the extraordinary adventures of this private investigator.

# The Strange Affair at Clifden

## CHAPTER 1

I have endeavored to put down on paper the details of the extraordinary events as they occurred. The years have not been kind to my memory and sometimes I am confused, and the recollections of those days are as I now remember them.

The letter arrived on the 10th. November 1953. The rain had been beating against the cottage windows since breakfast and it was so cold that I lit the turf fire at 11.00 a.m.

In the sanctuary of my warm front room I looked quizzically at the envelope wondering how my whereabouts had been discovered. At the top of the envelope below the stamp that depicted the recently crowned Elizabeth II my name and address were emblazoned in bold flowing writing:

*Jonathan Wilson,*

*The Cottage,*

*Near Mannane*

*County Galway Ireland.*

It was from Sedgewick Harris wishing me the compliments of the season and success with my book writing. I was surprised at the early wishes for Christmas, astonished he had traced me to my hideaway, and astounded he was aware of my writing endeavours.

I should have known better. Sedgewick Harris that exceptional student of mine from the Cambridge days, who was endowed with a brilliant analytical mind that astonished people. Such was his uncanny skill for problem solving that he became affectionately known as 'Sherlock'.

He had attracted the attention of the British Secret Service while at Cambridge and on the outbreak of World War Two was assigned to work on the Enigma Project at Bletchley Park. When the war ended, he set-up as a private investigator in rooms at Balfour Street, Mayfair, London. His reputation soon became the talk of that city and his exciting exploits even reached my ears while on an archeological dig at Luxor. It was said he had a photographic memory. I know that to be true.

*** 

My name is Jonathan Wilson, I am 6-foot-tall, sixty-two years old and slightly on the plumb side, unmarried and not in the least embarrassed by the extraordinary wealth left to me by my parents who tragically departed this life during the London blitz in 1942. Having no necessity to earn a living, no extended family and none of the constraints that inhibit others I am free to do as I wish. By nature, I am a solitary person and walking the quiet roads of this rural idyll is an absolute pleasure.

I had just returned from excavating in the Valley of the Kings and settled into my cottage near the village of Mannane a remote place hidden in the remarkable countryside of the west of Ireland. Here I would write and relive those past years in Egypt and maybe present my magnus opus to my old university where I had lectured for thirty years.

Every so often I venture to the village and visit Mannion's grocery store and sub-post office the nerve centre of the townland. Within this small emporium of faded colours the dispensing of groceries, whiskey, postage stamps and other necessities too numerous to detail takes place with kindness and efficiency. On the timber floor is stacked twine for binding hay, animal feed, bags of sheep dip and damp mysterious nameless faded yellow cartons.

The proprietress Helen Mannion is the recognised authority on all gossip and breaking news. In this Aladdin's Cave of wonderful fragrances of fruit and spice and black pudding the unfolding drama of the village and countryside is gathered and assessed before distribution to paying customers only. Like homing pigeons everything finds its way to the emporium.

Helen Mannion will forever be three years older than me, a significant age gap in those carefree summer days of long ago when as an innocent youth I spent my holidays with my parents at the cottage. It never seemed to rain then but it must have done.

The passing years have been kind to her. She is a striking elegant lady with a warm smile and radiant eyes. That compelling age gap that seemed substantial so long ago has with the passing of time become less significant.

A housekeeper Claire Noonan calls to the cottage every other day to look after essentials like cooking and cleaning. She lives with her bachelor brother Mike at Oak Tree Farm a twenty-acre holding further along the road. Of an age with Helen Mannion she is unobtrusive and down to earth. Possessed of that cute rural cleverness which I find so endearing she is another dear friend of those halcyon days. Her late mother helped out at the cottage in the earlier times. She was so pleased when I asked her to come in for a few days a week to look after me.

***

It rained for the remainder of the day and I retired to bed early. I lay there thinking of my friend, living as the letter indicated, in the dreary busy unfriendly streets of London. Was this a cry for help? Aware of the depression that afflicted him while at university I made up my mind to invite him for Christmas on the chance that he might come.

The following morning, I sent the letter and to my astonishment received a reply by return post requesting that he be collected the following Wednesday from the night train as he called it. Christmas Day was six weeks away and his early arrival surprised but did not disappoint me.

He strode imperiously up the platform his long coat flapping against his long legs. Clinched between his teeth was a Briar Pipe from which plumes of smoke rose almost enveloping his gaunt features. On his large head he wore a County Gentleman's Wilton hat, not unlike mine, it's brim turned down over his eyes giving him the appearance of a hoodlum. A few inches taller than me he was thin and stooped with the appearance of being undernourished.

Behind him a porter weighed down by two enormous suitcases scurried along to keep up. Here for the long haul I thought.

Despite the span of time since our last meeting there was no hesitancy in our recognition or greeting. The years had not diminished our regard for each other and as we sat in the back of the hackney car, we shook our heads in wonderment that we were together once more.

On and on the car went through the sleeping villages of Moycullen, Rosscahill, Oughterard and to the crossroads at Maam where it turned for Recess all the time heading towards Roundstone and a scattering of hamlets. Hidden among them lay Mannane and the cottage.

\*\*\*

That night we sat in the front room looking into the glowing turf fire listening to the howling wind. I had filled two generous glasses of Jameson whiskey-conversation sometimes needs a crutch to hobble it along. The delightful aroma of exotic tobacco invaded every corner of the room as Harris lay back in an armchair puffing like a train idling at a railway station.

'It was Fleming mentioned you were back in Galway.'

'Fleming?'

'You must remember? Red hair from the Scottish Highlands. Keen mathematics student back then. He is now attached to Scotland Yard.'

The memories flooded back, and I remembered the exceptional student with the heart of gold.

'How did you track me to the cottage?'

'Inspector Andrew Fleming and I meet quite often and on the last occasion he told me you had been seen at some of your old London haunts and the word was that you had returned from a stint in the Valley of the Kings. I was intrigued and wanted to meet you again. You disappeared but it was a small matter for me to figure out where you would go to record your archaeological endeavours. Mannane had been mentioned by you all those years ago and an enquiring letter adequately addressed found you.'

'How did you know I would retire here to write?'

'Jonathan you spend years in the Valley of the Kings scratching about on your hands and knees and all for what? Surely it was with the intention of writing up your findings and maybe you have considered presenting them to the old college?'

I was taken aback by the cleverness of his reasoning but then this was Harris. As the evening progressed and the contents of the Jameson bottle dwindled, we reminisced on days that had gone forever. He astonished me with stories of his time in London.

His account of the Beacon Hill Affair was remarkable and demonstrated his capacity to solve intricate problems that confounded everyone. I had read of the Hampton Court Mystery; it was in all the newspapers and was amazed that it was really Harris who disentangled an intricate problem that could have brought down Churchill's government. It would appear that Inspector Fleming of Scotland Yard consulted him frequently.

He did not explain that evening why after all the years he had sought me out but he looked tired and worn and I wondered if the dreadful illness still affected him. I was glad I had invited him. Here he could rest for a while. In my wildest dreams I never anticipated what would happen next.

# CHAPTER 2

The following morning, we set out at a brisk pace for Mannane. It would be a two-hour walk there and back. The village was quiet but the presence of Harris did attract some attention from the occasional passer-by, not because of his reputation, which had yet to reach the inhabitants of this rural backwater, but because the very fact that a stranger was among them was a talking point.

'Ah, there you are, Jonathan, just the man I was hoping to meet.'

It was Jones, a retired British Army Major who lived on the other side of the village.

'Major Jones, this is my good friend, Sedgewick Harris.'

'Ah, the famous Detective Harris with the remarkable powers of deduction. Is it true you have a photographic memory? Jonathan has told me everything about you.'

Harris, somewhat taken aback, looked at me questioningly.

I raised my hands and shrugged. 'Just said you were coming over from London and would be staying at the cottage. Maybe in passing I mentioned the uncanny abilities you demonstrated during your time at Cambridge, and the success of your private investigating practice in London.'

'Don't be too hard on Jonathan; your name was already familiar to me.

Heard it mentioned on a recent visit to the Reform Club of London, something to do with missing documents at the Foreign Office. Seen your name in *The Times* on occasion. Delighted to meet you. Wonderful!'

Harris had raised an enquiring eyebrow at the mention of the famous Reform Club and it was obvious to me that he was pleased he had been spoken of in such a prestigious establishment.

It is my opinion that every village should have a resident retired Army Major, preferably British. Now in his seventies, Jones had fought in both World Wars and returned home following each cessation devoid of outward scars. He was ramrod straight, somewhat on the boisterous side, honest and caring, and was a character I had admired from the first time I met him. He had a penchant for wearing loud tweed jackets, colourful cravats, cavalry twill trousers and stout brown brogues. His whiskey nose and lived-in face had hues of red white and purple and he was not unlike the White Rabbit in *Wonderland*, forever in a hurry.

'Must be off,' he said, despite having just met us. 'Things to do. You will of course be attending the painting exhibition in Clifden on Friday next, raising money for local charities. Have loaned them my Monet for the occasion. Must all pull together for good causes. Pick you up at 6.30. Glad that's settled.'

Off he went, whistling 'La Marseillaise' stridently through his teeth, a sign he was in a determined mood.

'It would seem we have just been invited to some exhibition in Clifden,' said an amused Harris.

*** 

Friday evening came, and so did the Major. We headed out the road to Clifden, listening to him extolling the virtues of his Monet, 'Sunset in Provence'. Harris stared, uninterested, out the side window of the car, his fingers tapping on the back of the seat in front of him. I could see that he was somewhat agitated. Perhaps the confined space of the car was disconcerting for him.

We arrived twenty minutes before the official opening and moved into the crowded hall to await the commencement of proceedings. The large and basic hall was cluttered with wooden chairs and tables. It was a functional place, not worthy of hosting a function. The shabby walls were covered in paintings of all shapes and sizes, no doubt submitted by local artists. They added colour. 'Sunset in Provence' had pride of place in a locked room adjacent to the main hall and would soon be revealed to the assembled masses.

Directly opposite us, free wine was being liberally dispensed by talkative, enthusiastic female volunteers. They were not short of clients who had come to view the Monet and partake of the wine that the parish priest had, by some devious means, managed to procure in Dublin. It was difficult to ascertain which the greater attraction was – a first viewing of the work of a famous artist or the opportunity to taste, for the first time, a drink many had only ever heard about.

At last, only twenty minutes late, the strident peal of a hand bell rang out and the chairman of the arts committee, Councillor Hubert Flynn, accompanied by a swaggering Major Jones, walked with determination through the hall in the direction of the room in which the Monet was hanging.

As they passed through the crowd, the Councillor waved a large key above his head to signal that the main event of the evening was imminent. Harris and I stood back from the moving throng that followed the large key. The Pied Piper sprung to my mind: *Brothers, sisters, husbands, wives, followed the piper for their lives*. The excitement was palpable.

Following a few words from the chairman during which the Major was thanked profusely for loaning his painting to the exhibition, proceedings began. The chairman inserted the large key into the big keyhole of the stout, brown coloured door and a loud click was audible as it was rotated. This action constituted but half the requirement necessary to gain access. The Major had another key, smaller but of no less importance than the bigger one, which he inserted into a lesser keyhole directly above the other one and turned sharply. He pushed the door and it swung open.

The assembled gathering, which, up to this point, had behaved excellently, now let themselves down. Not everyone was party to what followed.

Perhaps an over-indulgence of the inexpensive wine, which had been liberally served during the last hour or so, contributed to the unexpectedly boisterous conduct. Whatever the reason, there was a human surge through the door as soon as the Major opened it.

As is the way of all small village communities, the upper classes, as they would have viewed themselves, waited on the fringe and tut-tutted at the vulgar display of the lesser people. Harris and I stood aloof from all this. We know our place.

The clamour of those entering the room suddenly abated. An unnatural silence followed. Then a cacophony of sound invaded the small space. Something was amiss. The bewildered chairman exited the room and shouted in a loud voice, to no one in particular, 'The painting has been stolen! It is gone!'

Pandemonium, as people pushed to gain access to the room to view the blank wall. Horror, etched on the face of the Major. 'Someone, call the Guards!' he cried. Anxious faces all about, except for Harris, who was rubbing his hands in delight.

Eventually, two uniformed Guards arrived, and instructions were issued to close the exhibition. After much pleading and persuasion, the premises were cleared.

\*\*\*

'Baffled, that's it, I'm completely baffled!' The Major once more giving vent to his feelings, whilst clutching the steering wheel tightly. 'It's insured, but money won't bring it back.'

'Perhaps it will,' Harris replied with an enigmatic smile.

Did he know something? Surely not! Silence descended in the car and, save for the Major whistling a tune through his gritted teeth, not another word was spoken until we arrived at the cottage.

I insisted that the Major come in for a drink. 'It has been a stressful evening for you and a stiff drink, and a quiet chat will do you good.'

I gave him my armchair by the fire and pulled up a chair for myself. I filled the glasses with liberal measures of Jameson and built up the fire with sods of turf. 'Perhaps it might be helpful, Major, if you were to recount the events of the day.'

I looked at Harris. 'Are you interested?'

'Of course,' he answered as he went about the ritual of cramming tobacco into his briar pipe.

The Major, revived somewhat by the whiskey and the warm fire, began to speak though not in his usual clipped manner. Perhaps the recent shock had slowed him down.

'It seems like an age since Councillor Flynn and I locked the door to the room where we had hung the Monet. It was one o'clock exactly. I remember looking at my watch. Councillor Flynn had his key on a key ring and I had mine in my trouser pocket. The door can only be opened by these two keys and both of us would have to be there to do that. After we locked the door, we made our way over to the Foyle Hotel for lunch. We didn't meet again until I arrived at the hall with both of you, sometime before seven o'clock.'

Harris, who had been listening intently to the Major, asked, 'Was there anybody else present besides yourself and the Councillor when the door was locked at one o'clock?'

'Yes. Quinn and Smyth were talking in the corridor, just outside the door. They are committee members and had collected the painting from my house that morning.'

'Oh, I see. And what exactly occurred when they arrived at your house to collect the painting?' asked Harris.

'They arrived as arranged at 11.45 a.m. this morning and I carried the Monet to Quinn's car. The painting isn't big – it's twenty-eight inches by fifteen inches – and I sat in the back seat of the car holding it while Quinn drove. Smyth was in the front passenger seat. We arrived at the hall within twenty minutes and I carried the painting inside.'

'What happened then?' Harris asked eagerly.

'The three of us entered the room where the painting was to be displayed. A hook had already been screwed into the wall to ensure the most favourable eye-to-painting contact. This attention to detail is important when displaying quality works of art.'

'I'm sure it is,' said Harris. 'Were there many other people there to witness you hanging the painting?'

'Yes, quite a number. Everyone connected to the exhibition knew the painting was arriving and they came in to see it, maybe twenty people in all.'

'Did you notice any strangers among them?'

The Major hesitated for a moment and then he emphatically replied, 'No, most definitely not. I recognised everyone there.'

'So, you waited around until one o'clock and then you and the Councillor closed and locked the door and set off for the hotel.'

'Yes, we walked over to the Foyle.'

'Was the main entrance door to the hall still open when you left?'

'We were the last to leave and I pulled the door behind me. It locks automatically.'

'Where was everyone else?' Harris asked.

'They'd all gone to the hotel for lunch.'

'Everyone?'

'Yes, all the people connected to the exhibition had been invited to lunch by the local bank manager. You know how it is – banks tend to sponsor such local events.'

Harris was staring into the distance, his hands joined as if in prayer, visualising, I imagined, the scene the Major had so graphically described, or maybe it was something that had been said. One never knew with Harris.

He looked at the Major. 'It's such a pleasure to listen to someone who's able to sum up the events of the past few hours so succinctly. It makes a pleasant change.'

The Major was pleased at this. 'Would it be presumptuous of me to ask you to get involved in the case?' he asked.

'There's no need to ask. I think my presence this evening at the hall has already involved me. I will be keeping a watching brief for the moment and see how events unfold. It's a matter for the local Guards.'

'I'm much obliged to you for your kind, helpful words and grateful to you, Jonathan, for your hospitality,' said the Major, rising from his chair. 'I'm very tired; it's been an eventful day.'

I showed him to the front door and on the way to his car he said, 'Do you think Harris can solve this mystery?'

'I have every confidence in him,' I replied.

# CHAPTER 3

Saturday passed quietly without any news of the theft, and we spent most of the day indoors due to the inclement weather. The following morning, we walked to Mannane to collect the Sunday newspapers. The eleven o'clock mass had just ended and the congregation, having spilled onto the road, was in an excited, boisterous mood, dressed in their Sunday best and conversing cheerfully in small groups, as only good neighbours can.

Harris was mesmerised by the assembly of bicycles of varying shapes and sizes that were leaning haphazardly against the church railings, and all other available spaces. He was enthralled by the infectious excitement that pervaded not only the front area of the church but which spilled out all the way along the road right up to Mannion's emporium. 'It's truly wonderful! What I wouldn't give to be a part of this.'

On Sundays, two young girls came in to assist Miss Mannion. This was a big shopping day when the farmers and their families came in from the outlying countryside, not just to attend mass but also to stock up on provisions for the week ahead.

'Morning, Jonathan, how are you today?'

'Very well, thanks, Helen.'

Close to the bundles of newspapers laid out on the counter to facilitate the anxious, grasping hands were small bags of sweets piled high beside a handwritten sign which read *Aniseed Balls and Bulls Eyes, two pence per bag.*

They were immensely popular with the children, but the entire parish knew that Major Jones was their biggest customer. He never ventured out without one of the small bags in his pocket. The aniseed balls were his favourite, and if the wind was blowing in the right direction, it was possible to discern his approach, even from a distance.

Helen smiled as she handed me the newspapers which had been set aside for me. How radiant she looked, I thought, such elegance in so humble an establishment. I paid for the papers and as I walked to the door, I glanced back and caught her staring at me. She instantly averted her gaze.

***

Harris, captivated by the unfolding drama, had not entered the shop, remaining outside instead, intently watching everything. Eventually, I found him deep in conversation with Major Jones.

'Ah, Jonathan, how are you? I've being telling Harris about my conversation with Inspector Hennessy yesterday evening. Quinn and Smyth have been arrested on suspicion of stealing the painting. The audacity of them, collecting me on Friday morning, driving me to the hall with my painting, and all the time plotting to steal it!'

'That's splendid news. I hope you get it back before the day is out. Isn't it wonderful news, Harris?'

'Indeed it is, but I'm surprised matters have moved so quickly.'

'You have concerns at their arrest?' asked a puzzled Major.

'I've no doubt the good Inspector has his reasons for arresting the two gentlemen, but I had considered several other possibilities worthy of deliberation.'

'Was Inspector Hennessy wrong to arrest them?' enquired the Major, looking very troubled.

'Certainly not, he's working on an unusual case that has caught the attention of the national newspapers which, in turn, brings its own pressures. I'm quite certain his superiors are pestering him, demanding immediate results.

They're never happy when newspapers get involved.'

'Would *you* be interested in getting more involved?' asked the alert Major.

'Much as I would like to help in the ongoing investigation, it would be unprofessional to interfere in a matter that's in the hands of this Inspector Hennessy. It has nothing to do with me. I'm here to spend Christmas with Jonathan and could not countenance getting more involved.'

We said our goodbyes and as we turned and headed back to the cottage, we left a very pensive Major standing on the footpath, whistling through his teeth.

\*\*\*

Harris was pleased that among the many newspapers I took on a Sunday there were several English ones. We sat by the fire and settled in to wade our way through them. Miss Noonan had left a pot of stew simmering on the stove which we would partake of later in the afternoon.

'I knew it!' said Harris.

I glanced up from the paper. 'What's caught your eye?'

'There's an item here in *The Sunday Press* which states that a reward of £1,000 has been offered for the recovery of the painting.'

'Certainly a generous sum.'

'Indeed it is, Jonathan, a handsome figure. Strange the Major didn't mention it to us this morning. Surely he must have known?'

'There's something bothering you. What is it?'

'I have a dilemma, Jonathan, and it's not of my making. I'm here, as your guest, in this delightful country, removed from the annoying clamour and stress of London. Out of common courtesy to the police force here, I'm obliged to take a sideline seat, as it were, in the investigation. However, my observations of all that has happened over the past few days lead me to believe that there's a very devious, astute person involved in this theft. It would be a grave mistake to underestimate this adversary. The Inspector has made the cardinal error of moving too hastily. As I mentioned earlier this morning, the newspapers are stoking the fires and Hennessy has reacted to this by making the arrests. Had the press not been involved, he would have been more prudent.'

'But surely, when you have these misgivings, you must do something about it?'

'You're quite right, but it's not that simple. Were the events taking place in London then I could, without impunity, approach my friend, Inspector Fleming, at Scotland Yard and make him aware of my feelings. I have done that in the past.'

'Why not approach Inspector Hennessy and explain your predicament?'

'I think it would come across as interference. I have yet to meet him and he can hardly be aware of my work as a private investigator in London. I would be perceived as an interfering busybody, and an English one at that. No, I shall wait until he approaches me.'

'But that may never happen,' I said.

'Something tells me it will, and sooner than you think.'

*\*\*\**

It rained for most of the afternoon and I dozed in my armchair whilst Harris continued to read the newspapers. Miss Noonan had made enough stew to feed a dozen people and Harris and I unashamedly devoured the lot.

Suddenly the headlights of a car lit up the front room, even though the heavy curtains had been drawn. I sat up in my armchair, now fully awake.

'Whoever can that be at this time of the evening?' I said testily.

'Inspector Hennessy,' answered Harris, smiling and putting aside his newspaper.

I opened the front door and was confronted by a tall, handsome man, mid-forties I reckoned, with a mop of fair hair and the most amazing blue eyes I had ever seen. They seemed to stare into my very soul. His dark suit had a tired look about it but the white shirt was new and was perhaps being worn for the first time. However, it was the eyes that made this man. He looked at me inquiringly and said, 'I'm Inspector Hennessy. Sorry to drop in on you unannounced but I was passing close by on my way to Galway City and decided to call down.'

'You're very welcome, Inspector.'

'You're Jonathan?'

'Yes.'

'I thought so. I've seen you before, at Mannion's, in conversation with Helen.'

'Oh,' I replied, taken aback. 'Come in, Harris has been expecting you.'

'Really?'

'Yes, he's been watching out for you.'

We advanced to the front room.

'Inspector Hennessy,' I said.

'Delighted to meet you, Sedgewick, or should I say Harris? Everyone else seems to call you that. I've heard so much about you.'

'Don't believe everything the Major tells you; he's prone to exaggeration.'

'Yes, indeed, the Major did go on about you when he called to meet me at the barracks in Clifden yesterday evening but your name was already familiar to me. I have followed your exploits in the newspapers – you're highly regarded over here.'

Harris was well pleased at the compliment and squirmed in the armchair with a certain relish; we all like to be praised.

From the pocket of his jacket, Hennessy produced a twenty packet of Players cigarettes and placed one in his mouth. He struck a match, lit up and inhaled deeply. He then exhaled the smoke in the direction of the ceiling. He placed the cigarette packet and the box of matches carefully on the table beside him.

'I will come to the point,' he said, in his soft west of Ireland accent, as he settled himself into an armchair near the glowing turf fire.

'You're aware that I arrested Quinn and Smyth and can hold them until tomorrow evening at which time I'll either have to charge or release them.'

'Yes, the Major mentioned the arrest this morning.'

'The Major phoned me a few hours ago and intimated that you were surprised at my actions.'

'Somewhat, but then I'm not privy to your reasons for making the arrests.'

'It's pretty straightforward. Smyth and Quinn have come to our attention in the past but we've never been able to pin anything on them. They get involved in ventures that sail close to the wind, and when I learned they'd helped out with the exhibition, I decided to investigate further.'

He tapped the cigarette ash into the ashtray. 'The community hall is a busy place during the winter months. Several groups use it on a regular basis, and after a few enquiries, the local drama group came to my attention. They're rehearsing for their annual Christmas show, and on examining their list of members I came upon the names of Smyth and Quinn. They only joined a few weeks ago and I found that interesting as it coincided with the time the announcement was made that the Monet painting would be on view at the hall. On making further enquiries, I learned that some members of the drama group were surprised that they had joined and were forthright in their negative opinions of their acting abilities.'

Another plume of smoke was blown into the air. 'They rehearse twice a week at the hall, on Mondays and Fridays, and use the room from which the Monet was stolen as a storage area for props and costumes. That room is opened at the start of rehearsals and then locked when they have concluded. The keys to the room are then placed on a table in the caretaker's room. The caretaker comes in each weekday for an hour in the morning and maybe two hours in the evening. His duties appear to be nothing more than just being there. It's all rather vague.'

He took another slow drag of the cigarette. 'The opportunity was there for Smyth and Quinn to take the keys, probably on a Monday evening, a few weeks ago and to go to Galway or even Dublin to have duplicates made. They couldn't risk using the services of a local locksmith. They'd have had to come in early on the following Friday evening and leave them back on the caretaker's table. The room is only used by the drama group, so no one else would have been looking to use the keys during the other days.'

I marvelled at how methodical the Inspector was. He constantly referred to his notebook. Obviously it was written up to date and he explained things clearly and succinctly. He noticed things; even small, insignificant matters were not beyond his scrutiny and he displayed this trait in the manner in which he described them.

'So you think that sometime last Friday, after the Monet had been locked in the room, Quinn or Smyth used these duplicate keys to open the door, enter and steal the painting?' asked Harris.

'Yes. They could have sneaked in at any time in the afternoon. They were familiar with the layout and had assisted the Major in bringing the painting from his house.'

'I presume they deny any knowledge of the theft?' asked Harris.

'Yes, they are adamant they had nothing to do with it. I suspect the Monet has already been passed on to an accomplice who has the means of disposing of it. It's possibly out of the country by now.'

'I very much doubt that,' said Harris.

'I disagree with you. It would be extremely difficult for Quinn and Smyth to sell the painting in this country. How would they even know where to begin? I'm certain they had an arrangement with someone to take the painting off their hands as soon as they stole it.'

'Have you any thoughts on who that someone might be?' asked Harris.

'No, but it was common knowledge that the Monet painting was to be displayed at the art exhibition and there's always someone out there waiting for such opportunities. However, my immediate problem is that time is running out. Quinn and Smyth insist they never went near the hall after one o'clock last Friday, and that they remained at the Foyle Hotel all afternoon drinking after the sponsored lunch had ended. I checked their alibi and the staff at the hotel say they were there for all of Friday afternoon, but I'm not so sure of that.'

'I see. What do you intend doing next?' asked Harris.

'I was hoping you might be able to help me. The Major said you had some thoughts on the matter.'

'I do, but I will have to check out a few things first. I'll contact you tomorrow afternoon.'

'Are you hopeful of making progress?'

'Yes, I'm almost certain I know who stole the painting, but I would rather wait until tomorrow afternoon before divulging the name.'

'What! How could you know who stole it?' demanded the Inspector, almost choking on his cigarette smoke. 'You haven't even examined the scene of the crime.'

'Not yet, but the truth is in the news. Let's leave matters as they are for now and meet tomorrow afternoon,' suggested Harris.

I led a bemused Hennessy to the door.

*The truth is in the news* – what sort of idiotic talk is that?' he said as he stormed out the door.

# CHAPTER 4

It was Monday morning and the events of Friday evening were still the main topic of conversation. Harris relished the excitement of it all. That air of melancholy was gone and there was a sparkle in his eyes.

'I am certain that the key to the missing painting is to be found in Clifden,' he said.

'Would that be a big key or a small one?' I asked, tongue firmly in cheek.

'Jonathan, someday your quirky humour will be the undoing of you.'

'Sorry, Harris, I am unable to resist these moments of frivolity when an opportunity for wicked satire is thrust at me. It is a failing of mine.'

'It is by no means a failing but an admirable trait when used at the right time and place. Can we move on now?'

'Of course.'

'I have considered everything Inspector Hennessy told us yesterday evening, but he is most certainly on the wrong track. Let's walk over to Oak Tree Farm and ask Mike if he can drive us to Clifden today, preferably this morning. There are a few things I have to check out there.'

'Would you care to share your thoughts with me?'

'Later on, when we are finished in Clifden.'

\*\*\*

Mike had just returned from checking the cattle and was sitting on a window ledge, removing his muddy wellington boots. He was only too pleased to drive us to the community hall in Clifden. We were soon on the road and arrangements were made with him to collect us later that afternoon at the Foyle Hotel.

On our arrival in Clifden, Harris walked up and down along the front of the hall examining the layout of the ground and the large pot-holed car parking area. He stood with his back to the building and looked up towards the town. Directly in front was a row of tall, evergreen trees that obscured the rear of the houses that fronted on to the Main Street.

'Do you think the painting is still in Clifden?'

'Perhaps, Jonathan, but the solution definitely lies here.'

Our visit on the previous Friday had taken place in darkness and now, in the full light of day, I surveyed at first hand the exterior of the community hall. Some things are best seen at night time.

'This place is deserted, Harris, there is not a sign of anyone in the vicinity and I'm quite certain the entrance door to the hall is locked. How are we to get inside?'

'The necessity to enter the building does not arise. The answers I seek will be found outside, at the rear of the hall. Let's go, Jonathan, we will follow this path that leads around the perimeter of the building.'

I dutifully followed, trusting it was not a case of the blind leading the blind. How in heaven's name could the answers be found outside the building? Surely the solution lay within, where the robbery had taken place? But who was I to question the doyen of Balfour Street?

We followed the narrow path to the corner at the side of the building only to discover that it unexpectedly disappeared beneath a jungle of weeds and grass and trees.

'Oh dear,' said a perplexed Harris. 'Where has the path gone?'

*'It is underneath the coppice and heath*

*and the thin anemones, only the keeper sees*

*That, where the ring-dove broods*

*And the badgers roll at ease,*

*There once was a road through the wood.'*

'Once more, Jonathan, I am indebted to your superior intellect.'

'As I am to the words of Kipling.'

The wilderness stretched the length of the rear of the building and was a discouraging sight.

'I had not anticipated such a challenging prospect, Jonathan, but it is necessary for us to make our way to the window at the far end of the building. This is where the thief entered the room. It will mean traversing the entire length of this overgrown, neglected morass. We must tread carefully.'

'Would it not be easier to retrace our steps and go around the other side of the building and begin from there? We would come out immediately next to the window you have indicated.'

'You are right, but if my deductions are correct then this is the path the thief silently and deliberately came on his way to commit the crime. Had he entered from the other side he would have risked being seen by a passer-by. I noticed after we arrived and looked back towards the town that very tall trees obscure the view from all the houses that back on the hall except for one place. That place is the short road we came down when we turned off the Main Street. Anyone walking on that road has a clear view of the right-hand side of the hall as they proceed downwards. Our intruder could not risk walking around that side of the building as it left him open to the possibility of being observed by a passer-by.'

Once again, I marvelled at the keen observation of Harris; he noticed everything.

He moved cautiously forward, keeping close to the side of the building. I followed, trying to step into the prints he made but it was an impossible task. I could not match his long strides and so I gave up and ploughed my way forward. Progress was slow as not only had we to contend with the high grass, but we also discovered that the area had become a dumping ground for assorted household objects of varies shapes and sizes. Here and there were indications that the grass and weeds had been trodden down recently. Some person had been here lately.

We eventually reached the end window and stopped below. To our consternation, it was so far from the ground that it was impossible to climb up onto the window sill.

I felt truly sorry for Harris. All his deliberations, planning and assumptions had come to nothing. There was no way a person could climb onto that ledge and enter through the window. I watched as he contemplated this setback.

'I know that I'm correct, Jonathan, this is the way the thief gained entry to the room.'

He walked away from the window and made his way into the overgrowth. Suddenly there was an exclamation of triumph as he bent forward and extracted a small ladder from the high grass.

'You were fortunate to find that,' I said.

'It had nothing to do with fortune; I was looking for it.'

I could sense the excitement as he walked to the window with the ladder in his hands. 'Look, Jonathan,' he said, with intensity in his voice. 'See the indentations in the ground directly beneath the window.'

He placed the ladder on the ground and it fitted perfectly into the imprints that were already there. I had by now moved around and was standing beside Harris as he positioned the ladder and commenced to climb. In an instant, he reached the ledge and was peering through the window.

'Someone has climbed through this window very recently. There are scuff marks and bits of clay and grass on the ledge.'

He quickly began his descent. 'I have seen enough,' he said.

I was making my way back to the front of the building by the route we had come when a voice said, 'It might be easier to go this way.' I was mortified.

*** 

The lunch served at the Foyle Hotel was surprisingly good, and after our morning's exertions we were well ready for it. The young waitress kept watching us closely. I smiled at her and this gave her the courage to ask, 'Are you detectives down from Dublin to check out the robbery?'

I assured her we were not but, to my surprise, Harris eagerly engaged her in conversation.

'Most unusual thing to happen in a small town. Were you here on Friday when the painting was stolen?'

'Yes, I was serving drink in the card room and then moved in here to help with lunch.'

'The card room? What exactly is that?' asked Harris, suddenly alert.

'It's a room where the bridge club play twice a week, and it is sometimes used as a small reception area before people go into the dining room to have lunch or dinner.'

'And it was used on Friday?' he asked eagerly.

'Yes, the bank had a lunch here and everyone was asked to the card room for a drink before moving to the dining room. It's a handy arrangement for the kitchen as everyone is gathered in the one place and after the drinks they all sit down for lunch at the same time. It makes it easier for everyone.'

Just then a voice called from the hallway. 'Noreen, when you have time will you call into the kitchen. The chef wants a word.'

Harris, ever the charmer said, 'Noreen, that's a lovely name.'

'Thank you, sir, that's a very nice thing to say.'

To my surprise, Harris felt it necessary to acquaint the waitress with our names.

'My name is Sedgewick and this is my good friend, Jonathan.'

'Sedgewick,' she said mysteriously. 'Someone mentioned that name recently. I'm certain it was on Saturday afternoon. Sedgewick is a very unusual name. I had never heard it before and it stuck in my memory.'

She thought for a moment and then said, 'I remember now. I was folding napkins in the alcove under the stairs next to where the public phone is. I was not listening, but you can't help but overhear, especially if the person is talking in a loud voice.'

'And was the conversation all about me?'

'No. He said something like *Jonathan and Sedgewick do not understand how things are done over here and have no idea of the deviousness of holding.* These are the words I think I heard. I could be mistaken, but it is how I remember them.'

We were hanging on every word she said.

'Did he say anything else?' asked Harris.

'I think he said something like *you can be certain that the money will be paid. Don't worry, it will be all over within a week.* That is all I heard.'

Harris went very quiet. The news had unsettled him. He stared into the distance for a while and then asked, 'Do you know the name of the man talking on the phone?'

'No, but I remember seeing him at the bank lunch on the Friday. He was dressed in an odd manner. He was wearing a yellow-type jacket and had a small, coloured scarf tied around his neck and tucked into his shirt collar. I think it is called a cravat. He was very posh and walked like a soldier. There was a distinct smell from him, like aniseed ball sweets, if you understand what I mean?'

'The Major?' said a shocked Harris.

'It would seem so,' I replied.

Harris settled the bill and told the girl to keep the change.

'You are a very kind and generous man,' she said.

'And you are a very helpful young lady,' he replied.

*** 

Mike was outside leaning against the car when we came out. Parked next to it was the green, single-deck Connemara bus that had just arrived from Galway City.

'Why didn't you come in and join us?' I asked.

'The big sister warned me not to set foot in the hotel or any drinking establishment while I have the car with me.'

'Always listen to your sister.'

We had just pulled away from the hotel when Harris intimated that he wished to call to the Guards' barracks.

'Do you know where it is?' he asked.

'Yes, it's just up the road on the left-hand side,' Mike answered, driving towards it.

Harris went inside and was back in a few minutes.

'The Inspector was not there but I left a message for him to contact me,' he explained. 'We will head back to the cottage and hopefully he will call around later in the day.'

# CHAPTER 5

We were approaching Mannane and Harris, who, up to now, had been silently slumped in the front passenger seat, suddenly roused himself. He looked back at me and said in a quiet voice, 'We will call in and see the Major and get this over with.'

He then turned to Mike and said, 'Will you stop the car outside the Major's house, please. Don't bother waiting for us; we will make our own way home.'

The Major, as usual, was delighted we had dropped by and invited us into the front room. 'This is an unexpected but welcome visit. Would you like a cup of tea, or maybe something stronger?' he asked.

There was no response from either of us and I could tell by the way the Major looked in our direction that he sensed something was wrong. He had a puzzled expression on his face as he stepped away and moved to the window. He stood there with his back to us, staring out across the winter landscape.

'Why did you steal the painting?' asked Harris.

I was taken aback at the directness of the question. The Major spun around from the window and stared in disbelief at Harris.

'What has come over you, Harris? What are you talking about?'

'I know all about your telephone conversation at the Foyle Hotel last Saturday afternoon. You were overheard by a waitress who relayed everything she heard to me and Jonathan.'

The Major stood quietly in the centre of the room, deep in thought.

'Last Saturday,' he responded looking at both of us. 'Yes, you are correct, I met the Inspector in Clifden that afternoon and went into the Foyle for a drink. I did make a phone call while I was there. My heavens, is nothing private anymore? That conversation had no bearing on the recent theft of my painting.'

'That is not the way it appears to me,' Harris said. 'In the course of that conversation you were heard to say you did not understand the deviousness of holding on to something and that the money would be paid within a week, or words to that effect. Please tell me this is not true.'

I waited with bated breath. These were my best friends, caught up in a remarkable drama. What was unfolding before my very eyes was scarcely credible. There followed a short silence and then the Major spoke.

'You are the cleverest man I have ever met, Harris, but reliance on second-hand information can be fraught with danger. You, of all people, should know that. What the waitress told you is her interpretation of what she heard.'

'You did not steal the painting?' I asked, hope rising in my voice.

'No, I did not, don't be absurd. But I understand how easily you were led to that conclusion.'

Both of us watched him, waiting for an explanation that would hopefully prevent our friendship disintegrating. He stood ramrod straight and faced us down. He began to smile and then he laughed.

'Oh, dear Harris, did you really think I had stolen the painting?'

'I had to rely on the facts given to me. I came here immediately to ask you. I had to know.'

'The answer is very simple. The waitress put her interpretation on what she heard. She almost got it right. Allow me to graphically explain the meaning of her garbled translation.'

He walked over to the sideboard and returned with a pencil and a sheet of paper. He placed the paper on the table in front of us and, getting down on one knee, he began to write. We both read the writing as his hand moved the pencil across the paper. In neat handwriting were the words: *The deviousness of Holding is something else, but the money will be paid within a week.*

'Who is Holding?' asked Harris, immediately seeing the significance of the capital letter. I had not noticed it.

'Peter Holding is the local bookie. He owes a few of us a fair-sized sum of money for a recent flutter we had on the horses but he is refusing to pay out. Inspector Hennessy has taken the matter in hand and expects we will be paid within a week.'

'I hope you understand the reason I had to challenge you,' said Harris, with deep sincerity in his voice. 'I was certain you were not mixed up in this affair, but I am a creature of habit and everything, no matter how insignificant, has to be thoroughly investigated.'

'Don't give it a second thought,' responded the magnanimous Major. 'I understand completely why you jumped to that conclusion.'

'Interpretation of words can sometimes lead to grave misunderstandings,' replied Harris.

'Speaking of the interpretation of words, there is something that has been bothering me for some time now and perhaps you may be able to help me.'

'Yes, how can I be of assistance?' Harris replied, eager to please and regain some of the ground he had lost.

'I have a copy of *The Times* lying here for the past four days. It is sent to me once a week from a newsagents in Galway. I always attempt the crossword but have never yet succeeded in completing it; it's a devil of a thing. There is one clue in the latest edition and if I could just crack it I think I could complete the remainder of the crossword for the first time in my life. Wait a moment and I will get the paper.'

I just love the Major. Completing *The Times* crossword was perhaps a challenge for him but the ulterior motive was to offer Harris an opportunity to be of assistance and, in doing so, help to restore the friendship that might have slipped a little. How kind and thoughtful was that?

The newspaper was lying on his armchair, open on the relevant page. The Major offered it to Harris who said, 'Read the clue to me.'

'Surely you want to look at it?' asked the surprised Major.

'No, that is not necessary.'

The Major looked at him peculiarly and read out the clue.

'Number in theatre,' said the Major.

'How many letters?'

'Twelve.'

I watched in keen anticipation for I had seen him do this several times all those years ago. He spoke in a quiet voice so that we were able to follow his thought process.

'Number? One to a hundred? No! One who numbs? Maybe! Theatre? West End? Hospital? Yes. One who numbs in hospital theatre? Anaesthetist?'

He'd figured it out at the speed at which he had spoken. The Major was looking at him in admiration.

'They say that you can complete *The Times* crossword in three minutes.'

'Yes, but only on a bad day,' he replied.

# CHAPTER 6

The grey shades of the winter afternoon enveloped the countryside and save for a forlorn hen harrier swiftly winging its way home to the reaches of Lough Corrib, nothing else stirred. Harris was convinced Inspector Hennessy's arrival was imminent and I paced the kitchen, waiting for this confrontation when all would be revealed by the master of intrigue. The large car drew up outside, and through the window I watched the Inspector alight. I went to the front door to greet him.

'I got his message. Is it good news?' he asked anxiously.

'Perhaps, one never knows with him.'

'Inspector, how good of you to come,' Harris said, giving nothing away.

Once more the Inspector sat in my armchair. Visitors can be problematic; they sometimes feel they have rights.

'Did you have a good afternoon?' he asked, still anxious.

'Yes, the meal at the Foyle Hotel was surprisingly good, as was the waitress who attended to us.'

'The waitress?'

'Yes, a very observant young girl,' answered Harris.

'What has she to do with the matter at hand?'

'Everything; she unknowingly had the final piece to the jigsaw.'

'But have you a solution, Harris?'

'Jonathan, maybe three glasses of Jameson would be in order. Remind me to purchase a case when we are next in Galway City.'

I busily set to the task, whistling 'Jingle Bells'. If nothing else, I have a tune for every occasion. The call for the Jameson could only mean one thing.

'You will recall the moment I suggested the truth was in the news?'

'Yes.'

'You were lukewarm or rather skeptical with my observation.'

'It made no sense to me; I made that known to Jonathan at the time.'

'Indeed, he mentioned it to me but it made everything fit into place.'

'I still don't follow. What truth was in the news?' enquired Hennessy.

'A Sunday newspaper informed their readers that a reward of £1,000 had been offered for the recovery of the Monet and that added another dimension to my deliberations. What if the painting was stolen not to be sold but to claim the reward?'

The Inspector pondered this for a moment before answering.

'It's an interesting theory that has merit but makes little sense. The bigger reward for them would be in selling the painting. The Major informed me that it is worth £250,000. Quinn and Smyth had already asked the Major that question on first hearing it was to be exhibited. I have no doubt but am as yet unable to prove that they have sold the painting for a sum far in excess of the reward money.'

'My experience in the Tate Gallery Robbery some years back,' replied Harris as he reached for his pipe, 'copper-fastened my belief that it is one thing to steal a work of art but a different matter entirely to dispose of it. You even mentioned this the last time we met. If Smyth and Quinn did steal it, which I very much doubt, then it is still in their possession.'

'They don't have it; I'm certain of that,' the Inspector said.

'You are quite right, but the fact is they never had it because someone else stole it,' Harris insisted.

Hennessy started up from the armchair, almost spilling his whiskey. 'Who is it?' he asked with bated breath.

I looked over at Harris expectantly, knowing the answer would not be immediately forthcoming. I had observed him in the Cambridge days when that prodigious brain of his was called upon to unravel seemingly impossible problems. He responded with the solution almost instantly. I say 'almost instantly' for there was always a preamble, to allow the intricacies of the subject matter to be explained. When you solve a difficult problem that has baffled everyone else, the real glory is in the telling of the salient methods used to uncover the mystery. The solution is almost irrelevant.

'At first, I suspected the Major, but quickly ruled him out and yet I was looking for someone of standing within the community. Someone who would comprehend the complexities of stealing the painting and claiming the reward. That person would have to be aware the painting was insured and that the insurance company would offer a reward for its safe return. This narrowed the field to a few people.

'Having discounted the Major, I firmly fixed my attention on the real culprit but then I was completely thrown when new information came to hand. It indicated that the Major had stolen his own painting. Fortunately, it was all a misunderstanding. It was very unsettling and, for a short time, I even thought I was wrong in my deliberations.'

'Good heavens, you thought you were wrong.'

'Jonathan, we do not need, at this time, to be entertained with your sarcastic humour.'

I chuckled to myself and listened as he continued to speak.

'This morning, Jonathan and I returned to the community hall and inspected the scene of the crime.'

I watched the skeptical look on the face of the Inspector as Harris recounted the events of the morning that were still so vivid in my mind.

'So you never entered the hall?' asked the astonished Inspector.

'No.'

'How could you investigate the robbery without entering the premises?'

'My purpose this morning was to put my theory to the test and that did not necessitate entering the premises.'

'What you are suggesting is preposterous!'

Harris lay back further in his armchair. 'The scene of a crime is, of necessity, the first port of call for an investigator,' he said, 'but the real starting place is almost always somewhere else. The thief parked his car at the extreme left-hand side of the building last Friday, sometime before everyone went to lunch at the Foyle Hotel. He parked well away from the front door, aware that those leaving the hall would take the natural route that led onto the road. It was a good distance from his car – fifty yards or more.

'He would have sat in the car and kept his head down low and raised it, every so often, to peek outside and see what was going on. He eventually saw the Major lock the front door and head off with the Councillor. Exiting the car, he removed a small ladder from the car boot and moved quickly to the back of the building. In the event of someone seeing him, he would have said he was leaving the ladder at the side of the building for one of the committee members to collect.

'Like most people in the town, he was aware of the wasteland at the back of the building and would have come prepared. I'm certain he wore wellington boots. In less than five minutes, the ladder was up against the window ledge and he was in through the window, across the floor and had removed the painting from the wall. Ten minutes at most and he was back at his car. He placed the painting in the boot, removed his wellingtons and put on his shoes. He had already thrown the ladder into the undergrowth.'

'This is all very interesting, but purely speculative,' the Inspector said. 'May

I ask how the thief was able to enter through the window when it was locked? It would have been impossible without breaking the glass.'

'The window was not locked. Someone had left it open.'

'I'm sorry, Harris, but I must stop you there. The window was firmly closed when the room was locked at one o'clock on Friday last. It was one of the questions I put to the Councillor and the Major. The only way into that room was through the door and that is the way Smyth and Quinn entered.'

'Indeed, you are quite right when you say that it was locked when both these gentlemen checked it,' replied Harris, 'but someone else walked into that room just before one o'clock and discreetly pulled up the clasp that opened the window and gently pushed it out a fraction.'

'That is impossible. The Major and the Councillor would have seen this happen and they never mentioned anything when I spoke to them.'

'They did see someone in the room but because the person was one of standing in the community who had come in to convey an important message, they paid little attention to his activities.'

'What important message? No one mentioned an important message to me.'

'I am surmising, but I imagine he told them to hurry over to the hotel for their lunch as everyone was waiting for them. They would have thanked him, redoubled their efforts to finish off what they were about, and never noticed what he was doing at the window.'

'But how could the thief reach up to open the window? You told me yourself that you used a ladder to get onto the window sill?'

'Yes, but that was from the outside. The distance to a window from the floor is much shorter from inside a building. You must be aware of that?'

'The thief walked quickly to the Foyle Hotel and made straight for the dining room. I can imagine him looking about and asking one of the waiters to go out to the card room and tell everyone that lunch was about to be served. You have to give him credit for his meticulous attention to detail.

As the guests arrived at the dining room door, he was standing there to greet each one with a handshake and a few words of welcome on behalf of the bank.'

'The bank? Are you saying it was the bank manager? I don't believe it!'

'I suggest you suspend your disbelief and return to Clifden and interrogate the manager before he mysteriously finds the painting and claims the reward. That would be awkward. Ask him to open the bank's safe so that you can look inside.'

Hennessy sprang from his chair, shouting his farewells as he rushed out the door.

***

The following day, it had just gone three o'clock when the Inspector returned to the cottage. I opened the door and he entered, carrying a case of Jameson.

'It would be a disaster were we to run out of this stuff,' he said.

'A calamity,' replied Harris.

'You are very kind, Inspector. There was no need for you to go to such expense.'

'It's a small token of appreciation, Jonathan.'

Hennessy looked at Harris and, in a measured voice, he began to speak. 'Everything was as you said it would be – the painting was in the safe as you predicted. He confessed right away; was a real gentleman about everything. The unfortunate man has a serious gambling habit and has being stealing the bank's money for years to feed his addiction.'

***

The pale winter sun brightened the snow-covered fields and made shadows behind the stark, bare trees. It had been three weeks since the Monet Affair and Christmas Day would soon be upon us. I had booked Harris, the Major and myself into the Great Southern Hotel in Galway City for the duration. I noticed Harris' mood swings and was concerned that he was slipping into that dark abyss that visited him every now and then.

As if reading my thoughts he said, 'I love this place, Jonathan, and could stay here forever.'

It grieved me to see how sad he was.

'What has brought all this on?' I asked.

'I will be returning to London in the New Year to reopen my Balfour Street rooms. It is time I went back.'

'Do you want to go back?'

'No, but I live for the adventure, Jonathan, the chase, the sheer thrill of it all. I need that to function properly. I must be doing things. The Monet Affair was exhilarating but it will be a long time, if ever, before something like that occurs here again.'

As is often the case in the midst of a serious discussion, some idiot will intrude, and the moment is lost and that last step is not taken. I hurried to the door to answer the intrusive knock. Why now of all times?

'Sorry to disturb you, but is he in?'

'Yes, Inspector, in the front room.'

'Ah, Harris, hope it is not a bad time.'

'No.'

As was usual with Hennessy, he came directly to the point.

'So sorry to impose on you, but I am involved in a case that is causing me untold problems. I need some help and was hoping you would come to my aid.'

'What sort of case is it?' asked a somewhat interested Harris as he reached for his pipe.

'It's an incredible one and you will find it difficult to believe what I am about to say. It happened yesterday evening at a golf club near Louisburgh in County Mayo.'

'Louisburgh?'

'Yes.

'But, Inspector, what can have happened in a small golf club that is so incredible?'

'Let's just say that what occurred is of such significance that my superiors in Dublin have taken a keen interest. The Commissioner, aware of your involvement in the Monet Affair, has suggested I consult you as a matter of great urgency. Will you come to Louisburgh with me? I would not ask you unless it was important, but maybe this is a bad time?'

'Well, Harris?' I enquired, almost afraid to ask.

He looked at me for a moment and then suddenly jumped out of the chair.

'Get the coats and hats from behind the door, Jonathan.'

The chase was on.

# Murder at Louisburgh

## CHAPTER 1

It was bitterly cold that December afternoon, in 1953, with the threat of snow as I walked out of the cottage, my head bent low against the wind, and made my way towards Inspector Hennessy's car. An early darkness had descended and enveloped the countryside but, despite all this, the air was crisp and clean. At the request, or perhaps I should more accurately say, the insistence, of the Inspector, Harris and I were about to embark on a journey to a remote golf club located near the village of Louisburgh in County Mayo.

Harris was leaning against the bonnet of the car, maintaining his balance with one hand while he deftly tapped his briar pipe against the heel of his shoe with the other. These duties at an end, he sat into the front seat and I watched him take the leather tobacco pouch from his overcoat pocket and set about filling his pipe. From experience, I knew this would be a lengthy process and at its conclusion a decision would be made as to whether or not to go to the next stage. I hoped he would not take that step as the prospect of a smoke -filled car was something I could definitely do without.

My great coat was buttoned up and I was flushed with anticipation at what lay ahead. I was like a schoolboy heading off on an outing. Never before had I seen Hennessy so determined and I could hardly wait for him to explain precisely what had happened at that remote golf club.

\*\*\*

I wrapped the Foxford rug around my legs and settled myself in for the journey. Experience had taught me never to rely on the heating system of a motor car. Hennessy, in the driver's seat, glanced back at me, checking perhaps to see if I was comfortable. He started the engine and the car drew slowly away from the cottage and headed in the direction of the village.

Harris was still occupied with his briar pipe and every now and then he would glance over at Hennessy with a questioning look. Finally, he could take no more and asked, 'What is this great matter of urgency at Louisburgh that has everyone in a flap?' I noticed the superior manner in which Hennessy looked at Harris. It was one of those *I know something you don't know* looks. In such situations, one has to be careful not to antagonise the expectant listener.

For a moment, I thought the Inspector was not going to answer, and just when I was about to give up on him, he said, in a cool, steady voice, 'A man was shot dead at the Western Golf Club near Louisburgh yesterday evening.'

It was the casual nature of his tone that gripped my attention. He said it in such a matter-of-fact way, as if he was used to imparting such news, but I knew that a shooting in the west of Ireland was a rare event and wondered if the Inspector was attempting to be nonchalant in front of Harris; trying to impress him, as it were.

'What?' exclaimed Harris, impressed and deeply shocked at what he had just heard.

I, too, was stunned by the statement, but managed to ask, 'Was it accidental?'

'Maybe, but I don't think it was. The information I have is vague and incomplete but I do know a robbery was in progress at the time. There is a witness to the event, the caretaker of the golf club who resides in a small flat adjacent to the clubhouse. Apparently, he heard a noise during the night and went to investigate. When he entered the premises, he was confronted by two men, one carrying a rifle and the other a trophy that had been taken from the club's trophy cabinet. I believe the trophy – a gold cup – is very valuable. A confrontation took place, and in the ensuing struggle one of the intruders was shot dead. That is as much as I know, but I will be brought up to date when we get to Louisburgh. I have arranged to meet the forensic people at the clubhouse.'

We were passing the Emporium and I glanced over at it, hoping to catch a glimpse of the proprietress, Helen Mannion, but there was no sign of her. Harris had observed my action and was shrugging his head and throwing his eyes to the heavens. He was not a ladies man.

'Why in heaven's name would a valuable gold cup be on display in the remote Western Golf Club?' asked Harris.

'The same thought struck me,' answered Hennessy. 'Are any of you familiar with the game of golf?'

Harris shook his head to indicate his lack of knowledge and I answered, 'No.'

'The golf club and course have been closed to the public since the incident was reported which means that there will be no club members at the location when we arrive. That is unfortunate as it would be helpful if we could get speaking to even one of them.'

'I think we will be able to speak to one of the club members today,' I replied.

'Oh,' said Harris, turning around sharply to look at me.

'Major Jones is a member of the Western Golf Club; he told me as much some time ago and we will be passing his house in a few minutes. I think we should stop and pay him a visit. I'm sure he will be willing to assist us and perhaps we should invite him to come to Louisburgh. It would be helpful, as you said, Inspector, to have someone with us who is a member and familiar with Golf Club.'

'You may be certain he will be willing to accompany us,' agreed Hennessy. 'It wouldn't surprise me if he has not already made his way over there. He has a tendency to turn up in the most unexpected places, poking his nose into everything.'

'It's just his curious, generous nature,' I replied, defending my friend's propensity to be somehow always at the scene of the action.

***

Hennessy pulled the car over to the side of the road and stopped outside the neat bungalow that was home to our friend, Major Jones. We got out and walked up the short driveway to the front door. It swung open and there stood the smiling Major. He was wearing a red and green check shirt, open at the neck, with a yellow cravat that had blue and green stripes. His fawn cavalry twill trousers were supported by bright red braces. On anyone else such outlandish apparel would look ridiculous, but on the Major it was sheer perfection.

He bellowed at the top of his voice, 'This is a wonderful surprise. Am I worthy of such a visitation? Three wise men calling!'

'We were just passing,' answered Harris, 'and on an impulse decided to call and say hello.'

I looked at Hennessy in astonishment. Just called to say hello? At times, I despaired for Harris. Why not state your real business and get on with it, I wondered. The Major was nodding his head in a knowing fashion; he knew we had come looking for him.

'Passing by? Are you on the way back from or over to Louisburgh?' he asked, smiling.

'You know about the incident?' asked the astonished Inspector.

'The whole country knows about the murder.'

'Murder! Who said anything about murder?' exclaimed a shocked Inspector.

'Brendan, the postman, gave me an update when he delivered my letters a short time ago. His sources are generally very reliable. The word in the village is that it was murder, but why are you wasting valuable time calling on me? Surely I can't help you?'

The Major was something else, as they say. He knew quite well that our call was more than a social one and I do believe he was taking pleasure at seeing Hennessy in a tight corner.

'We are on our way to the golf club now and we were hoping you would come with us in your capacity as a member of the club. We need someone to show us the ropes, as it were. Someone, like you, who plays the game and is familiar with the set-up and the daily goings-on, and Jonathan suggested you,' replied Harris.

The Major looked at me and said, 'I would do anything for Jonathan.'

'I was sure you would,' replied Hennessy. 'I must be off now. I have arranged to meet the forensic team at the clubhouse and I might even catch the pathologist if I get a move on. Major, would you oblige me and drive Harris and Jonathan to Louisburgh later on? I really must get on the road.'

'Of course, I would be only too pleased to oblige.'

***

Following the Inspector's departure, the Major brought us into a bright front room that faced towards the distant Twelve Pins Mountains. We adamantly refused the offer of whiskey and settled, out of politeness, for a cup of tea. Tea was poured from a silver teapot. Rarely had I seen so much Wedgwood on a silver tray; the Major had class.

'Have you read the account of the robbery in this morning's newspaper?' he enquired. 'There is a brief report in the breaking news column on the back page.'

'No,' replied Harris. 'Could I see it? I find that newspaper reporters who are under pressure to meet a deadline have a precise way of expressing themselves that is always relevant and to the point. They tend to capture the moment in a succinct way and it is the reason I invariably glance at that back page first.'

'But they can sometimes be generous with the truth,' I said.

'Indeed, no one is perfect.'

The Major handed the newspaper to Harris and, for my benefit, he read it aloud.

*The prestigious Sir John Redford Gold Cup was stolen from the clubhouse of the Western Golf Club in County Mayo last evening. The trophy first, played for in 1906 by the leading amateur golfers in Connaught, is said to be priceless. It was on display in a glass case on the club premises. Some time yesterday evening, the secretary of the club, a Mr John Morgan, heard a disturbance and came to the door of his flat to investigate. From his doorway, he could see lights flashing in the clubhouse windows and went to inspect the premises. Several gunshots were fired and there are unconfirmed rumours that one of the intruders was shot dead. Another intruder made off across the golf course with the gold cup. Inspector Hennessy is leading the investigation. An arrest is imminent.'*

'What do you make of that, Jonathan?'

'I am pleased to hear that an arrest is imminent.'

'Jonathan, if an arrest was soon to be made, the Inspector would have mentioned it. The newspaper reporter was just using a tried and trusted sentence to close off his article. But what has happened is very unusual. This is not the usual modus operandi of a rural thief. Rarely do they carry firearms. This smacks of a city gang.'

'I am inclined to agree with you,' said the Major as he stood at the window, holding his teacup.

'Did the postman have anything further to add to the story?' asked Harris.

'Not really; though he did hear that the secretary, John Morgan, was extremely brave and put his own life at risk.'

'And nothing else?'

'No.'

'This Sir John Redford Gold Cup,' I said, 'is it really very valuable?'

'Yes, Jonathan, it is said to be worth thousands of pounds. I have a tenuous connection to it, you know – won it in October 1939. Two months later, I found myself in Cherbourg, en route to the Maginot Line to play my part in the Second World War. It now seems so long ago. Never did get the celebration.'

'Celebration?' asked Harris. 'What do you mean?'

'It's a very old tradition, rooted in the turn of the century,' replied the Major as he poured more tea and placed a plate of currant buns on the table.

'In August 1906, Sir John Redford presented the trophy to the golf club. There were certain conditions attached and the main one was that it would never leave the premises and would always be on display in the clubhouse.'

'And the celebration? What exactly is that?' asked Harris.

'Sir John's birthday is the 28th day of October and he stipulated that, on that day every year, a dinner would be held to celebrate his birthday and the triumph of the winner of that year's competition. The gold cup, as decreed by him, was to be taken out of the display case and carried in ceremony by the officers of the club and placed on the table in front of the winner. The celebrations would then commence. At midnight, the ceremonial party would reform and return the trophy to its case where it would remain for another year.'

'What a wonderful tradition!'

'It is, Jonathan, but because of the outbreak of war, and the fact that I was away fighting, the celebration was not held. I never did get to hold the real gold cup. But I do have a replica of it which was presented to me on the actual evening I won the competition, in August 1939.'

The Major excused himself and left the room for a few minutes. When he returned, he was carrying a replica of the trophy he had won on that summer's day so long ago. It was, I estimated, approximately ten inches high and about eight inches in diameter; not unlike the chalice used by clergymen in a church. Despite a lapse of fourteen years, it was still in reasonable condition, somewhat stained and with a few dents but, all in all, a presentable trophy.

The Major proudly handed it to me and I admired it for a few minutes before passing it over to Harris.

'What a lovely trophy and a wonderful story,' he said, handing it back to the Major.

'It will be getting dark soon and I think we should make our way to the golf club and take a look at the scene,' suggested Harris, as he stood up from the table.

\*\*\*

Harris sat in the back of the car and I got in beside the Major. Beyond the village of Leenane, we crossed into Mayo and its wild, rugged beautiful countryside, all the time heading toward the southern part of Clew Bay and the village of Louisburgh. There were stunning views out across the Atlantic, with outlines of numerous islands visible.

'Over there is Clare Island, one-time home of the Pirate Queen Grainne O'Malley,' the Major said, pointing to a vague outline shrouded in the mist of the wild Atlantic.

\*\*\*

The entrance to the golf course was so unimposing that a stranger would surely have driven past. Two small sand dunes, one with a windswept sign planted on it, indicated that we were at journey's end. Major Jones guided the car between the dunes and drove up to the front of the clubhouse where he stopped and parked next to the few other cars that were there. We got out and I stood, looking at the clubhouse. It resembled an old pavilion that had fallen on hard times but still had something magical about it; an oasis in an isolated place on the western coast.

'Where does the secretary live?' enquired Harris, immediately going into action.

'In that small flat over there,' the Major replied, pointing to a building further down from the clubhouse. 'He is not the secretary; the club does not have one. He is a caretaker.'

'I see,' murmured Harris, taking his pipe from his great coat pocket. He proceeded to light it as he walked away. 'I will be back shortly. There is something I have to do.'

With that, he walked down the short incline towards Morgan's flat.

# CHAPTER 2

I noticed Hennessy had parked a little further along, to the side of the clubhouse. He was more than likely inside with the State Pathologist and the team of forensic people. From my understanding of these matters, I reckoned it would be sometime tomorrow before any results would be available. The front door to the clubhouse was cordoned off and a uniformed Guard stood there, preventing anyone from entering.

On the journey over, the Major had explained, in a concise manner, the management structure of the golf club. We learned that most golf courses had eighteen holes but the one we were going to had only nine holes. It was interesting to hear that the club membership was in the region of fifty men and fifteen women. A small number, it seemed to me but the Major went on to point out that not too many people played golf in the area and the number, whilst appearing low, was respectable.

Most members played at the weekend and a small bar was opened to serve drinks for a few hours. Any member playing during the weekdays just came and played their round of golf, and went home. The changing or locker rooms were open for a few hours during the weekdays but everything was locked up at 5.00 p.m. from the months of October to April.

A visitor coming in for a casual round of golf, a most unlikely event at this time of year, would be directed by a sign at the front door to pay the green fee at the caretaker's flat. The entry or green fee was placed in one of the envelopes provided, in a black tin box, which was on the window ledge of the caretaker's flat. The visitor would write his or her name on the envelope, enclose the fee, seal it and drop it into the letterbox in the door. These instructions, whilst appearing convoluted, actually worked

The summer months were when most activity took place. Competitions were held every Sunday during that time. The Major told us that, at this time of year, there was little activity and on some days no one at all turned up to play.

*** 

The Major and I walked around the side of the clubhouse and came to the golf course itself. It stretched away in the distance towards Clew Bay. We then strolled back to the front of the clubhouse and stood there. Down by the caretaker's flat, I could see Harris with his hands thrust deep into his long overcoat pockets, staring intently in the direction of the clubhouse. I watched as he crouched down and began to work his way slowly towards us, his gaze fully focused in my direction. It would not have surprised me had he got down on his hands and knees and crawled. When you were in the company of Harris, anything was liable to happen.

Just then, Inspector Hennessy emerged from the clubhouse, accompanied by an older man whom I took to be the State Pathologist. They shook hands, and the pathologist, for it was he, got into his car and set off down the driveway. I managed to overhear his parting words: 'I will phone you later tonight with a preliminary report. It will take a few days to get the final one out to you.'

'Ah, Jonathan, good to see you. Major, I meant to ask you earlier on if you still had that Monet hanging on your wall?' We laughed politely at this reference to the recent Clifden Affair.

'Where is Harris? Is he not with you?'

'He is, but he's down near the caretaker's flat walking about and behaving strangely,' I answered.

'Nothing new in that,' remarked Hennessy.

With that, Harris came around the corner of the building and, on seeing Hennessy, said, 'there is something very odd about this robbery.'

He took his pipe from his pocket and stood looking out towards the distant Atlantic seas. Then he turned around and asked, 'Any news on the missing gold cup?'

'Not yet, it is still early days, but I'm certain it is somewhere in the area.'

'Really?' said Harris.

This, I thought, was an unusual thing to say. I looked in his direction and frowned. He smiled back at me in a conspiratorial way. Was he on to something? Just then, the door of the clubhouse opened and two men carrying cases and large paper bags emerged.

'Looks like the forensic people have finished,' said Hennessy.

'Can we go into the clubhouse now?' asked Harris.

'Of course you can. I'm just popping over to say goodbye to the forensic people and will follow you inside shortly. Be careful, the body of the unfortunate intruder is still lying on the floor where he fell.'

*\*\**

We made our way through the main door and into the clubhouse. From the tiny foyer, a long corridor stretched all the way to a door at the very back above which was written *First tee to the right.*

A bit further on, and no more than halfway down the corridor, lay the remains of the unfortunate intruder, covered by a long white sheet. Now that the pathologist and forensic people had gone, I assumed a vehicle was on its way to collect the body and bring it to the morgue. It was a disturbing scene.

The corridor was dark and untidy and in need of a good cleaning. At one time it must have been a pleasant place, but the passing years and maybe the scarcity of funds had taken their toll. From a wall that at one time must have been painted a vivid green, a broken trophy cabinet hung at a precarious angle.

Harris, as was often the way, seemed to sense my thoughts and said, 'It is a pity we could not get Miss Mannion, our housekeeper, over here for a few days, Jonathan. She would smarten the place up. Does anyone ever attend to the cleaning here, Major?'

'Morgan, the caretaker, looks after that, but I see what you mean. It needs a woman's touch.'

The Major pointed to a large varnished timber board that was screwed into the wall on the left-hand side as one looked down the corridor towards the back door.

'That is the Sir John Redford board on which is inscribed, in gold lettering, the names of all the winners of the gold cup.'

He walked over to it and proudly pointed his finger at the line which read Major RH Jones 1939. Harris stood in front of it for a few minutes, shaking his head, in appreciation, I imagined, and then turned away and walked to the back door, muttering to himself.

Hennessy came in and informed us that an ambulance was on its way to collect the body and would arrive in a few minutes.

'I think we should go outside and let them do their job,' he suggested.

***

It was a relief to be out in the fresh air, away from the distressful scene we had just witnessed. Harris, who, up to this point, had been preoccupied, turned and addressed Inspector Hennessy.

'Before you go, Inspector, there is one thing I need to ask you – where is John Morgan, the caretaker? I knocked on the front door of his flat but there was no answer.'

'I understand he is staying with his sister in Leenane, some ten miles out the road. The poor fellow must be in a state of shock,' answered the Major.

Feeling I had to contribute something to the conversation, I asked, 'Has the body been identified yet?'

'Not yet,' replied Hennessy, 'but I am confident we will soon have a name. I am surprised the local Guards have been unable to identify the victim, which indicates to me that the man was a stranger and not from this area.'

'How about you, Harris, have you formed any opinions on the matter?' the

Inspector asked, hopefully.

'There are several things that strike me as odd and there is something about this crime that is just not right, but I can't work out what it is at the moment. These matters will become clearer when I speak with John Morgan.'

'I will contact you tomorrow and give you an update on Morgan's condition. Hopefully, the preliminary report from the pathologist will also be available by then.'

The Inspector then turned to me and said, 'Jonathan, would you get on to the telephone people and demand that they install a phone in your cottage immediately? It is very time-consuming for me to have to drive from Galway City every time I wish to speak with Harris.'

'Believe me, I have been trying to get one since I arrived here in September, but it will be another three years before they can do anything. One of the drawbacks of living in the country, I suppose.'

'Surely not a drawback,' said Harris, as we walked towards the Major's car.

# CHAPTER 3

On a good morning when it was not raining or too cold, I would stand in the front garden and look across the fields all the way to the Twelve Pins Mountains. It is an exhilarating view. I would watch the rolling clouds sweep the morning light across the ever-changing countryside, altering the landscape to greys and greens, as far as the eye can see. In my mind, I'd imagine the quiet, hidden villages and the people going about their daily work and would be envious.

Harris had been up and about since early morning and was sitting in the front room, still in his dressing gown. He could be irritating at this time in the morning, but he had one great redeeming feature – he knew how to light the fire. Even at this early hour, it was essential to have a good fire blazing. The smell of the burning turf that pervaded the entire house was soothing and wonderful.

He had been intrigued by our visit to the Western Golf Club and even though we had arrived back to the cottage very late the previous evening, he had not gone to bed. Instead, he sat in his armchair mulling over the events of the day. I had peeked surreptitiously over the top of my *National Geographic* every now and then and observed his strange behaviour. He had set down a big sheet of white paper on the small table in front of him and, with long strokes, sketched some sort of map with a pencil, or so it seemed.

'It makes no sense.'

'What makes no sense?'

'The car.'

'What car?' I asked.

'The car that was not there.'

This was all too much for me; it had been a long day and I decided it was time to retire to bed. I left him, still talking away to himself.

I did not hear him retire that evening and was most surprised to find that he was up and about before me the next morning. As was usual with me in the morning, I went to the kitchen to make a pot of tea. Harris followed me and stood looking out the window before he turned to me and mumbled, as if embarrassed, 'Happy birthday, Jonathan.'

I was staggered by his greeting. Seeing my confusion, he said, 'I don't have too many friends but the ones I have are very dear to me, and it is but a trifle to remember important dates.'

Maybe it was a trifle to him, but to me it meant so much more.

***

The kettle was bubbling loudly on the hob and I was keeping a tight eye on the toast. The trick was to have the tea just drawn and ready to pour as the toast popped up; a feat that constantly eluded me. Hearing the sound of a car, I looked out the window and saw Inspector Hennessy alighting. Must be important to bring him around so early, I thought. Opening the door, the tea and toast now in turmoil, I bid him a good morning and ushered him into the front room to the warmth of the fire and the presence of Harris.

I soon joined them with offerings of strong tea and slightly burned toast. They ate it, regardless.

'I promised to call to you as soon as I had any news, and it so happens quite a lot has gone on since we last met. The pathologist was on to me first thing this morning and told me what I already was more or less aware of – there was just the one gunshot, which proved fatal as it entered the victim's chest and heart. He would have died instantly.'

'I see,' replied Harris.

'You mentioned something yesterday, Harris, at the golf club that puzzled me and which has preyed on my mind since.'

'Oh, and what was that?'

'You mentioned, in passing, that there was something not right about the robbery. At the time, I took it as a throwaway comment, a mere conjecture uttered in general conversation.'

'Believe me, Inspector, I never utter mere conjectures. My comments are always relevant and should never be taken as throwaway statements.'

The Inspector, duly admonished, nodded his head.

Harris, taking his pipe from the ashtray, continued.

'It is no ordinary robbery. I am puzzled by the fact that the burglars brought a rifle with them. Surely, in an isolated place like the golf club, it would not be necessary to carry a firearm to steal something from a trophy cabinet? It makes no sense.'

'Yes, I agree with you, and I apologise for my tactless choice of words, but I am under pressure from headquarters. Chief Superintendent Coveney is constantly on to me.'

'No need to apologise, I understand.'

'I came over to give you the latest news from the pathologist, but something more remarkable happened earlier this morning, at the morgue. Believe me, when this gets out the newspapers will have a field day. It will make the headlines in every newspaper here and maybe even overseas.'

Hennessy proceeded to butter a slice of toast, leaving his words hanging in mid-air.

'But what is this remarkable news?' enquired Harris in a cranky voice.

I looked at Hennessy in an expectant way, knowing that he was holding back on his news just to annoy Harris. It was an old ploy of his, used now and then, that gave him the satisfaction of knowing he knew something Harris did not.

'This morning, at the morgue, one of the attendants, a local man and a member of the Western Golf Club, saw the body and had no difficulty recognising it but was shocked when he realised who it was.'

Hennessy took his twenty pack of Players cigarettes from his pocket, opened it and took one out. He struck a match and lit the cigarette.

Harris was not amused by these antics and I was surprised that the Inspector was resorting to such childish tactics. If you have something to tell, then say it, I thought. Eventually, Hennessy looked over at Harris and said in a dramatic voice, 'The body was that of a priest from Castlebar.'

'Aha!' exclaimed Harris, smiling, 'Father John Flynn, I presume?'

Never in all my life have I seen a person more astonished than Hennessy was. He stared at Harris in utter disbelief; he was speechless.

'How could you know that name? I, myself, was only informed of it an hour ago.' He struggled to contain his composure. 'The name has yet to be released to the general public, but yet you knew it. How can that be possible?'

A smiling Harris rose from his chair and said, 'I must get dressed. I will be back shortly and will head over to Louisburgh with you. I have to meet John Morgan. By the way, did you locate the car yet?'

Out the door he went, singing, in a fine baritone voice, a piece from *The Pirates of Penzance*. *'I am the very model of a modern Major General; I've information vegetable, animal and mineral.'*

The voice faded away and Hennessy sat there, mouth open, still speechless, a slice of toast held in mid-air.

'What car is he talking about? How in God's name did he know the name of the priest?'

All rhetorical. I was used to the vagaries of Harris. He remembered my birthday when I thought that no one in the whole wide world, outside of myself, knew; was aware of the priest's name even before it came into the public domain; but singing a song from The *Pirates of Penzance*! Where would it all end?

# CHAPTER 4

Walking out the door of the cottage, the notes of that song still dancing in my head, I was immediately embraced by the icy chill that had arrived during the night from faraway Siberia. Even though I was well wrapped up in my heavy overcoat and thick woolen scarf, they were little match for this cold invader. Snow was forecast for later in the evening. Harris was impervious to the weather and, I do believe, whether it was mid-summer or mid-winter, it made little difference to him.

I shivered as Hennessy drove the car along the deserted road towards the southern tip of County Mayo. The heater in the car seemed to be blowing out cold air and my feet were freezing. The mention of Father John Flynn, half an hour earlier, had caused such a sensation that I had forgotten to take my Foxford rug with me. There was no way I could ask Hennessy to turn the car back.

'Harris, you must tell me how you knew the unfortunate victim lying in the morgue was Father Flynn. How in heaven's name could you know that?'

'All in good time, Inspector. There are more pressing matters to attend to this morning and number one on my list is John Morgan, the caretaker. Will he be at his flat? It is important that I speak with him as soon as possible.'

'I made it clear to the Guards in Louisburgh that I wanted to meet Morgan today at the golf club. I expect him to arrive later on.'

'So you have not yet spoken to him? Has he made a statement?' asked

Harris.

'No, I have not spoken with him but he did make a statement earlier this morning. I was in telephone communication with a Guard in Louisburgh a few hours ago and he relayed a general outline of the contents of it. There was nothing of significance. Obviously, it was a theft that went dreadfully wrong.'

'Perhaps you would be kind enough to share your information with Jonathan and myself, no matter how insignificant it may seem to be. There are so many unusual things about this case and every scrap of information, no matter how unimportant it may appear, would be helpful,' remarked Harris.

'Well, as I already told you, the Guard had very little new information to relate. In fact, the newspaper reports have more or less covered the events as they unfolded. Morgan says he was dozing in an armchair in his flat, around six o'clock that evening, when something woke him. He opened the door of the flat and stood looking towards the clubhouse. He could see a light flickering along the widows inside the building. It was obviously the light from a hand torch.'

'Was he still standing at his front door or had he moved outside and gone towards the clubhouse?' Harris asked.

'I don't know, but surely it is not important?'

'Everything that happened that evening is important.'

'I understand that, but I have not spoken to him yet and am relying on third-hand information. From what I'm told, he made his way over to the main entrance of the clubhouse and entered through the front door.'

'Was the front door locked?'

'I don't know, but Morgan would have had a key to gain entry. You will recall, from your visit yesterday, that once you enter the clubhouse you are able to see from the front door all the way along to the back door. As soon as Morgan entered, he could see two people walking towards him from the direction of the back door. The lights were not on but one of them was holding a torch, which gave a small amount of illumination.

'In the dim light, he was unable to see their faces but was able to make out that one of them was holding the Sir John Redford Gold Cup while the other one had a rifle. With incredible courage, Morgan charged at the one holding the rifle and wrestled with him. In the ensuing struggle, the rifle went off and killed the person holding the gold cup.'

'Oh!' exclaimed Harris, taken aback at these stark words.

'Then what happened?' he asked.

'The intruder hit Morgan on the shoulder with the rifle, picked up the gold cup and ran out the back door. Morgan staggered after him and saw him running up the first fairway with the rifle in one hand and the gold cup in the other.'

'He was a very foolish man to pursue someone with a rifle,' suggested Harris.

'I'm not sure if he actually pursued him. I think he followed him for a short while to get an indication of where the thief was running to, and then he went back to his flat.'

'Well, Inspector, it is all a question of perception. For my part, in a similar situation I would have bolted the back door and the front door, and may even have ducked under a table for safety.'

'And you, Jonathan, what would you have done if you had been there?' asked Hennessy.

'I would have been under the table with Harris.'

'I see. You are well matched, the pair of you. However, to continue, Morgan was terrified that the thief might return so he raced back to his flat and locked the door. He immediately phoned the Guards at Louisburgh and eventually, just before 8 p.m. that evening, two Guards arrived at the scene. The local doctor arrived very soon after that. The doctor pronounced the man dead and prepared to return to Louisburgh. He examined Morgan's shoulder and gave him some painkillers.

'One of the Guards phoned the headquarters in Galway and informed a Superintendent of the killing and robbery. It was by now coming up to 9 p.m. and the Superintendent told the Guards to remain at the scene until a forensic team could be dispatched to them. He also informed them that the State Pathologist would arrive later the next morning. The doctor very kindly went out of his way and drove Morgan to Leenane and dropped him off at his sister's house before returning to Louisburgh.

Harris had gone very quiet and I could see he was running all this information through his weird brain.

'I would like to see a copy of that statement at some time, if that is possible. You said the contents were not significant but I find what you have just relayed to be intriguing and worthy of further examination.'

'Maybe, at a later time, I will be able to do something for you, but would you please tell me how you knew that Father John Flynn was the name of the person shot dead? For the life of me, I can't understand how you knew that. Only a few people were aware of this.'

*** 

Harris had his unlit briar pipe firmly clenched between his teeth and removed it to answer the Inspector's question.

'All crime scenes have a central focus point which tends to attract too much attention. To me, the body lying on the floor, covered by the sheet, was of little significance, but I noticed that you and Jonathan were immediately drawn to it. Acute observation and detailed examination of the entire crime scene is what matters in an investigation. The fact that the back door was not only locked but had a bolt drawn across it was of interest to me, yet that fact has never been mentioned by anyone.

'But to address your immediate question concerning the identity of Father Flynn, the answer to that was no more than three feet away from where the body lay, in full view for everyone to see.

'Really? I don't follow,' said Hennessy.

'On the wall beside the cabinet that contained the gold cup there is an honours board on which are listed the names of all the previous winners and the year they were victorious. You must have seen it, I'm sure? Everything is handwritten in gold lettering, a wonderful piece of craftsmanship. The Major's name, as he pointed out to us yesterday, is there for the year 1939. The winner this year,1953, was Father John Flynn. Among all the names listed on the board since 1906, he is the only reverend gentleman, but there are two others with the name Flynn – one in 1912, the other in 1949.'

'How could you remember all those names on the board?' asked the puzzled Inspector.

'I just stored the names in my head.'

Hennessy stared in disbelief at Harris, wondering how he did that. I knew how he did it; I had been witness to the workings of his photographic memory on many occasions.

'At the time, that name had little significance until you mentioned this morning that the victim was a priest. There cannot be that many priests who would be frequenting the Western Golf Club. I concluded that, in all probability, the priest who was shot dead was Father John Flynn. I could have been wrong, but that rarely happens.'

'Interesting reasoning,' said the Inspector, 'but it still makes no sense to me. A priest attempting to steal the gold cup? It is scarcely believable.'

'Exactly my thoughts, Inspector, but the priest was not trying to steal the Sir John Redford Gold Cup; he was attempting to put it back.'

# CHAPTER 5

We rounded the corner of the golf club entrance and drove into the car park that had been deserted the previous day but which was now overflowing. We had difficulty finding a space but, eventually, with the aid of a Guard who was on duty and who recognised the Inspector, we got one.

The wind was howling in from Clew Bay and, in the distance, across the fairways and sand dunes, the churning of the sea could be heard. Members who had not set foot in the place since late summer were back in their droves, attracted by the notoriety and events of the last few days. They had come to see the place where the shooting had happened but there was really nothing to see. Some had even travelled long distances. On this exposed headland of Clew Bay, the only place to be was the Western Golf Club.

The tiny bar to the side of the long room where the robbery had taken place was capable of accommodating no more than thirty people, and the overflow of interested onlookers had taken to standing in every other available space. At a guess, I imagined that the full membership was present. The barman, who obviously recognised Hennessy, came from behind the counter and said, 'I suggest you go down to the far end of the clubhouse, to the locker rooms. You can sit in there. It isn't too comfortable but it will be quiet and you will have somewhere to sit and talk. I will send some tea and biscuits down to you shortly.'

\*\*\*

We sat in the bleak locker room on a hard bench that ran around the perimeter of the place. True to his word, the barman arrived with three mugs of tea already filled with sugar and milk, and a packet of biscuits. Not the Ritz, but I think we all appreciated his gesture.

'At least we can talk here. Is there anything in particular you want to discuss, Harris, before I go over to interview Morgan.'

'Oh, he is back then?'

'Yes, the Guard at the front door told me he arrived about fifteen minutes ago.'

'You go and speak to him first, Inspector, and following that we will decide the next step. There are a few more things I have to check out. But, tell me, do you have on your person, or do you know where to obtain, a list of the contents found on the body of Father Flynn?'

'I do not have an actual copy of the list but I copied all the items listed into my notebook for future reference.'

The Inspector was meticulous in his note-taking; this instance was a case in point and proved his attention to detail. Nothing was left to chance and I had no doubt he was destined for higher places. He reached into his inside pocket, took out his notebook, opened it and began to read.

'A rosary beads, twelve shillings and four pence, a set of keys, a tie pin. Then there was a leather black wallet containing the following items – a library card, a sheet of paper on which is written a list of times for upcoming masses, an invitation to a forthcoming wedding, and a receipt for one shilling from a jeweller's shop in Castlebar.'

'Is there a date on that receipt?' Harris asked.

I immediately noticed the intense excitement in his voice.

'December 2nd,' replied Hennessy.

'Interesting,' said Harris, 'just a few days ago.'

'I'm going over, now, to speak with John Morgan at his flat,' said the Inspector, getting up from the hard bench.

'Jonathan and I will take a look at Father Flynn's car. It is parked where it was yesterday and I noticed, when walking past, that it was still not locked.'

'I will go and speak to Morgan and catch up with you later.'

'Alright,' replied Harris.

*\*\*\**

Once outside, Harris went over to the priest's car and began a thorough examination of it.

'Are you looking for anything in particular?'

'I'm looking for things that are not in the car.'

'What? I don't understand? How can you look for something that is not there?'

'It is a skill given only to very few; a gift.'

Was he having me on? I refused to continue any further with this line of conversation. Harris had his ways and they could be eccentric, outlandish; even downright crazy. But looking for things that were not there was a first, even for him.

He was smiling at me and shaking his head. 'If you could only see the look on your face,' he commented

'Please tell me what you are doing.'

'We have to assume that Father Flynn came here to play golf.'

'Yes, I should imagine so. Why else would he drive all the way from Castlebar? It is twenty-five miles from here.'

'Well, then, where are his golf clubs? They are not in the car. I have been looking for something that is not there.'

'They could be in the locker room.'

'No, I checked when we were sitting there a short while ago but I will look again.'

He stood beside the car and stared into the distance towards the Atlantic. I watched, transfixed, as he went into a dream-like trance. He was doing exactly the same thing he had done earlier with the list of names on the honours board.

Suddenly, he turned to me and said, 'There are six sets of golf clubs in the locker room. One has the name William Browne attached to it on a bronze disc and the others have plastic name tags attached to them. I can see the names – Brannigan, O'Reilly, Mannion Jones, and Coen. There is an odd assortment of golf shoes scattered about, but they are not relevant to this case. There is nothing there that belongs to Father Flynn.'

His weird photographic memory had taken a picture of the locker room while we had been seated there and now he had revisited it to look at the names. I said nothing. What was there to say?

'There is no sign of Father Flynn's clerical clothes, either in his car or in the locker room. It leads me to believe that he was still wearing them when he was shot dead. If he had played golf, he would have put on his golfing clothes and changed again when he was finished. There are no clothes in the locker room or in his car. It is obvious, Jonathan, that Father Flynn did not drive over here to play golf. The question is why did he come?'

'Have you any idea what that reason might be?' I asked.

'Yes. I have already mentioned that I am convinced he was trying to get the gold cup restored to the trophy cabinet, but I need more information to back this up.'

'I imagine that will be difficult,' I said.

'Perhaps, but the receipt from the jeweller's shop is interesting and merits further investigation. If only we could find that other car. I don't think it exists and that would explain why it can't be found.'

'You are confusing me, Harris. What is this car you are hoping to find but think does not exist? It does not make any sense to me.'

'Jonathan, according to Morgan, there were two people in the clubhouse yesterday evening – the priest and the other intruder, who ran off. Father Flynn had arrived by car some time before the robbery and parked outside the clubhouse. How did the other intruder get here? If he came by car, it should be still parked here. On that first morning, when the Major drove us over, there were five cars in the car park. They belonged to Hennessy, the pathologist, the forensic team, the Guards, and, as we now know, Father Flynn.'

'Perhaps the other intruder sneaked back after he ran away up the first fairway, got into his car, and drove off.'

'No, Jonathan, Morgan was locked in his flat but could still see out the windows to the car park. Within half an hour, the Guards arrived and took over. There was no way a car could be driven away without being seen.'

'So where is the thief who ran up the fairway with the rifle and gold cup?'

'He has been hiding in the same place all the time.'

'What place is that?' I asked

'In Morgan's head, Jonathan. There was no second intruder; he never existed.'

# CHAPTER 6

We were still standing beside the priest's car when the Inspector came round the corner.

'Did you find anything interesting in the car?' he asked.

'Enough to point me in a meaningful direction,' replied Harris. 'How did your interview with Morgan go?'

'It was straightforward. He is still a bit confused, which is only to be expected after all he has been through.'

'And you are satisfied that he had nothing to do with the robbery?'

'Yes I am satisfied', replied the Inspector.

'Do you think the priest was involved in this crime?' asked Harris.

'He must have been, but it does not sit well with me. Not the sort of thing one would expect from a clergyman. I told Morgan that you would be calling down to see him. He is a bit shook up but is fully coherent.'

'George, the barman told me there is a fine hotel in Leenane where we can get a good meal,' Harris stated. 'I suggest we go there for something to eat and to discuss our plan of action for the afternoon. I find it difficult to concentrate when I am hungry.'

'Are you not going to speak with Morgan? Was it not the main reason you came here today?'

'That can wait for now, he is not going anywhere. I would much rather eat before I talk with him.'

***

When we entered the Leenane Hotel, a turf fire was burning brightly at the far corner of the bar. Like a magnet, it drew us to the small table and chairs that were arranged close by. Harris insisted that we sit here and have a drink before ordering our food. It was a bit early for me to be drinking whiskey and I felt duty bound to let the others know my feelings.

'I never drink whiskey until the evening time, as a matter of principle, but if both of you are that way inclined, then I will join you in just the one.' I felt much better having made my position clear. Their silence was an indication to me that a drink would be acceptable. 'We will have three Jamesons, please,' I called out to the barman.

'I so admire a man with principles,' remarked Harris, smiling mischievously and taking his pipe from his pocket. The Inspector was opening his packet of Players cigarettes while frisking himself for his box of matches.

***

I can still vividly remember that time in the Leenane Hotel as Harris recounted to Hennessy and me the extraordinary saga of the missing gold cup and the tragedy that was such a dreadful part of it.

'It all has to with Father Flynn. He was the unwitting instigator of all that has occurred in the last few days. We must go back to October 28th last, when he was presented with the gold cup at the celebration dinner at the clubhouse. You will recall Major Jones relating to us the ceremonial aspect of the evening? When the gold cup was presented to Father Flynn, he would have held it aloft for a few minutes in triumph and then set it down on the table. At the stroke of midnight, the gold cup was returned to the trophy cabinet.

'There the matter should have ended, but something happened that evening that concerned the priest. He went back to his parish in Castlebar and tried to put the matter behind him. The weeks went by but the anxiety he felt still bothered him. He finally made up his mind to meet the problem head on. He went to a jeweller's shop in Castlebar, on the pretext of buying a tie pin, whereas, in fact, he was seeking something else. He was looking for information which only a jeweller could provide, and he got that, I am certain, without causing any suspicion. When he walked out the door of the jeweller's shop, he had his mind made up on the course of action he was going to take.'

Hennessy and I were hanging on to every word. Such was the excellence of Harris' delivery that I had already consumed my whiskey but, because of my so-called principles, felt unable to order another. I glanced around the table in the hope that someone might understand my predicament. No one did, or, if they did, they pretended not to notice.

'What happened next?' I asked.

'He telephoned Morgan at the golf club and arranged to meet him the next afternoon. Father Flynn may have mentioned the gold cup and, in all probability, he did. When he arrived at the clubhouse the next day, Morgan was waiting for him at the front door. Father Flynn would have said he wanted the gold cup taken out of the cabinet so that he could hold it in his hands. Morgan had the key to the cabinet on his key ring and he opened it. The priest would have reached in and removed the gold cup and held it in his hands for a few minutes. He had to be certain.'

'Certain of what?' asked a bewildered Hennessy.

'Certain that what he was holding was the gold cup.'

'I don't follow,' I said. 'Surely it was the gold cup?'

'No, it was a replica, just like the one Major Jones showed us yesterday.'

'A replica?'

'Yes.'

'So, where is the real gold cup?' I asked.

'After the Major won the trophy in 1939, the war years intervened and it would be another three years after the war ended – 1948 – before it was played for again. Morgan is a greedy man and, during the war years, when little or no golf was played and he had barely any income, he saw an opportunity to make some money.

'The price of gold was on the rise and reaching astronomical figures. It was a mean time in a world that was at war. The black market had become almost the norm throughout Europe and anything could be bought or sold without questions being asked. By some means, Morgan encountered a contact that was willing to buy the gold cup from him. The deal was agreed and the gold cup was removed from the clubhouse.

'To cover his tracks, Morgan went and bought a replica cup from the company that had supplied them over the years. He probably told them that the competition was being played that summer despite the fact that the war was still raging. This would have been in 1941 or 1942. If you contact the suppliers, I am certain they will verify that.'

'How did Father Flynn know that the gold cup was not genuine?' I asked.

'On the night of the celebration dinner, in October, when he was handed the gold cup, he was surprised that it felt so light. Remember, he had been presented with the replica last August when he was announced as the winner. He was immediately suspicious that something was wrong, but he had to be careful about making accusations. At this stage, he had an open mind and went away to think about it. The more he thought about it, however, the more he became convinced that the cup in the cabinet was a replica.

'He went to a local jeweller and asked questions about the weight of gold compared to gold nickel. So as not to arouse the suspicions of the jeweller, he bought the tie pin, and in the course of that transaction, he learned enough to convince him that the gold cup in the trophy cabinet should be much heavier than the replica he had on the mantelpiece in the presbytery. He was certain they were more or less the same weight which meant that the gold cup was not real, but a replica.

'We will never know what happened at the encounter in the clubhouse that evening, but Father Flynn may have said he was getting the Guards involved, or reporting the matter to the golf club committee. Morgan would have pleaded with him to let it go and not report it. I imagine the priest, being a God-fearing man, insisted that the theft would have to be reported.'

'But to kill a man? That is so incredible. Why did he do that?' I asked.

'Morgan had a lot to lose. Once the news broke of the gold cup being a replica, he would lose his job as caretaker and the wages that went with it, as well as the free living quarters. He would be arrested for robbery and perhaps spend time in jail. Being caretaker, or secretary of a golf club, as he preferred to be known, carries a certain amount of prestige, and he stood to lose all that. As a last resort, he shot the unfortunate Father Flynn.'

'He must have had the rifle in the clubhouse or brought it with him in an attempt to frighten the priest,' said the Inspector. 'It means the killing was premeditated.'

'Inspector, that will be for a court of law to determine. It does seem a drastic thing to shoot a man, but I think he panicked,' said Harris.

'When did you first suspect Morgan?' I asked.

'Five minutes after we arrived at the clubhouse on that first morning,' he replied.

 I could see that Hennessy was shocked to hear this pronouncement by Harris.

'How could you have known within five minutes?' asked the Inspector.

'When we stopped at the Major's house that morning, he showed us two things – his replica of the Sir John Redford Cup and the morning newspaper. One should not always believe what they read in newspapers but, on this occasion, I believed what I read to be true. In the article on the robbery, it stated that, *From the door of his flat he saw flashing lights in the windows and went to investigate.* I believed that statement to be true as no newspaper reporter would make that up.

'When we arrived at the golf course that morning, I immediately went down to the front door of Morgan's flat and looked towards the windows of the clubhouse where he had seen the flashing lights. There are no windows on that side of the clubhouse. He had never seen any flashing lights.'

'You suspected him immediately?' asked the Inspector.

'Yes, but I had to gather more evidence to prove it. There was the matter of the trophy cabinet. If the thief, as suggested by Morgan, smashed the glass in the cabinet to steal the gold cup, why were there no shards of glass lying in the bottom of the cabinet? It would be natural that there should be.

'I believe Morgan opened the cabinet with his key and took the cup out and handed it to Father Flynn. Maybe he still had hopes that the priest might be confused and say that the whole thing was a mistake on his part, and that the cup was the real Sir John Redford Gold Cup. But that did not happen. Father Flynn would have told Morgan, in no uncertain terms, that he was going to report the matter to the golf club committee.

'The prospect of being arrested and put in jail was too much for him and, in a moment of madness, he shot the unfortunate priest. To cover his tracks and pretend that the trophy cabinet had been broken open by the intruders, he set about smashing it with the rifle. However, a few minutes prior to that, he had opened the cabinet door with his key to take out the gold cup, which meant that the small glass door was swinging open. When he broke that glass, it fell all over the floor. I noticed there was no glass in the bottom of the empty cabinet, but there should have been if the cabinet had been smashed by the thieves when it was locked.'

Then there is the matter of the back door which was locked and bolted the first morning we arrived.

Morgan said he chased the intruder out that door and then turned back and locked himself into his own flat. Who locked the back door? No one. It was never open because Morgan never ran out through it.

'You have done well, Harris, I think it is time I took Morgan into custody.'

'Yes, that is the thing to do; I have no interest in speaking to him now.'

Harris beckoned to a waiter and asked for the lunch menu. Hennessy stood up from his chair and said, 'I won't be joining you; it is time I went and arrested Morgan.'

'Very well,' answered Harris. 'Perhaps you might send someone over in a few hours to drive us back to the cottage.'

Hennessy, in the course of lighting a cigarette, nodded and went out the door.

*\*\*\**

' I don't think the inspector appreciates all you've done; does it not bother you?' I asked Harris.

'Not in the least; this is my way of life. It is what I live for and it brings me many compensations. During my time in London, I was busy but there was a feeling of isolation. I was on my own in a big city. Here, in this wonderful place, I have found that I am gradually becoming part of the community.

'Financial reward is not an incentive anymore. My years as a private investigator in Balfour Street in London were rewarding in many ways, particularly from a financial standpoint. I am in receipt of a generous annual stipend from Her Majesty's government in recognition of my services to the Foreign Office. They still have a call on me should that requirement ever occur.'

'So, you might have to return to London?'

'Yes, Jonathan, from time to time, but you can always come over with me and stay for the duration. I value your company and, most of all, your quirky sense of humour. But have no worries, I will always come back to Mannane.'

*\*\*\**

It was late afternoon when the car arrived to take us back to the cottage. I loved these journeys on the quiet country roads that traversed this beautiful unspoiled countryside. Christmas would soon be here and I was looking forward to the few days away with Harris and the Major in the Great Southern Hotel in Galway.

The car slowed as we came to a crossroads and Harris pointed to a signpost and said, 'How do you pronounce that name?'

'Oughterard,' answered the driver.

'What a lovely name. We must go there someday,' suggested Harris.

'Yes, why don't we do that,' I replied.

At that moment, I wasn't to know that our next adventure would take us to that beautiful village to investigate the sensational Mysterious Room in Oughterard.

# The Mysterious Room in Oughterard

## CHAPTER 1

I had taken to walking to the village of Mannane on my own. It was not by choice but, rather, because of the difficult circumstances that prevailed between myself and Harris. There had been a few demanding days when he'd watched for the postman or Inspector Hennessy's car in hope and expectation. An immediate stimulus of sorts was urgently required to bring him back from that cursed melancholy that preyed with a vengeance on his mind when inactive. He had to be doing things.

The Enigma Project during the last war was an antidote that brought him five years of quiet contentment. The dreary fingers of despair never touched him then and, at that time, in that place at Bletchley Park, under relentless pressure and with the lives of so many dependent on him and all those others, he had met each day with confidence and determination.

I scarcely noticed the grazing cattle and sheep in the fields that stopped to look up and stare at me as I walked by. I was lost in my own little world, wondering whether or not my friend would take off and return to London. Rounding the sweeping corner that gives the first aspect of the village of Mannane, I was immediately struck by the unusual activity outside Mannion's shop and sub-post office. The Emporium, as I affectionately called it, was owned by the lovely Helen Mannion. She was a dear friend of mine from the old days.

A crowd was gathered; there must have been at least five or six people, an exceptional congregation on a Friday morning. Major Jones was prominent among them and he was agitated. He saw me, detached himself from the assembly and made strides in my direction.

'Where is Harris?' he shouted, as he approached. 'Why is he not with you?'

The distance between us shortened and I could now speak face to face with him. 'He is having one of his not-so-good days and decided to remain indoors,' I replied.

The Major nodded in sympathetic understanding. He was aware of the illness that beset Harris. Although they had only met a few months earlier, on the day of the Monet robbery, in fact, there was an unusual bond between them. Who could not like the colourful, outlandishly dressed Major with the loud voice and exemplary manners? I watched closely as he chewed on an aniseed ball sweet whilst stroking the side of his ear in reflective contemplation.

'Hmm,' he said to no one in particular before turning to me.

'It's a pity, Jonathan, that he is not here, on this morning of all mornings, as he would be truly astonished to hear of the unbelievable events that occurred at Oughterard yesterday evening.'

Oughterard is a bigger village than Mannane and lies some thirty miles east of Clifden, close to Maam Cross. It is said that when you cross the humpbacked stone bridge over the Owenriff River at Oughterard, you are entering the fairyland that is Connemara. It is a sleepy place and I was mystified by the Major's remarks.

'What unbelievable events?'

'The break-in at the village bank. It was robbed during the night and a vast quantity of money was stolen. They were saying in Mannion's that it could be the biggest robbery ever in the country.'

'Did you say country or county?'

'Country.'

I could only smile at the Major's exaggeration, and he immediately noticed my condescending attitude.

'Some things are not always as they seem and I quite understand your sceptical reaction but, believe me, you will comprehend the true significance of the event when you hear the full story.'

He paced back and forth, whistling through his teeth. His words had a profound effect on me, and I instantly thought of Harris back at the cottage, slumped in his armchair, brooding. Had I just been presented with an elixir that might rescue him from his condition? Much as I was eager to hear the Major's tale, I desisted, and said instead, 'Do you have your car with you this morning?'

'Yes, it is parked over there,' he said, pointing. 'Why do you ask?'

He was somewhat peeved that I had interrupted his train of thought; his annoyance was reflected in his slightly raised voice.

'I was hoping you might drive me back to the cottage and join myself and Harris for tea and baked scones that have been made freshly this morning by our excellent housekeeper, Miss Noonan. He would be so interested to listen to your account of the robbery. My version could never match yours – you have such a wonderful, eloquent way with words.'

This pleased the Major no end; he straightened himself to his full height and swaggered and strutted as we walked towards his car. On opening the car door, he turned to me and, smiling in a wry way, said, 'There was no requirement, Jonathan, to flatter me. I would do anything for Harris.'

\*\*\*

I sat into the car and the Major drove away from the village in the direction of the cottage.

To my surprise he said, 'Did you ever think of buying a car?'

I was taken aback by the suddenness of the question and replied, 'Why would I want to buy a car? I don't even know how to drive.'

'That can be soon remedied. Just think of the freedom you would have. You could buy a brand-new Morris Minor for £475 in Galway City.'

'I will give it some thought,' I replied.

'I'm thinking of changing my car and, if you were interested, I could sell it to you at the very good price of £200. You could then learn to drive for a few months and trade it in when you are buying a new one. You are so isolated out here in the country and, as I already said, it would give you more freedom to move about. Why don't I loan you this car for a few days and you will be able to practice your driving on the quiet country roads.'

'We will talk about it tomorrow,' I answered diplomatically. I mulled over the idea as he drove steadily down the narrow road. Perhaps he was right; maybe I would buy his car and learn to drive.

# CHAPTER 2

On entering the cottage, I called out to Harris. 'Guess who I have brought back with me!'

'Let me see. Who is that person who drives about in a noisy car that disturbs the entire countryside and can't refrain from poking his nose into everyone's business? Is it by any chance the Major?'

The Major was coming in the front door and heard everything. I was mortified but needn't have worried; the old soldier rose to the occasion with dignity.

'Good morning, Harris,' he said, 'still as acerbic as ever. Some things never change.'

'Ah, Major, how good of you to drop by. Please forgive my rudeness, but it has been a difficult few days.'

'Nothing to forgive; I understand. Delighted to see you.'

I just loved the way the Major spoke in rapid, short, meaningful sentences. Every word was a prisoner with him. It warmed my heart to see such magnanimity in the face of the unwarranted slight. Would I be so forgiving and generous in a similar situation? I hoped I would be. The preliminary greetings, such as they were, being at an end, I directed the Major to an upright armchair directly opposite the one in which Harris was slumped. I sat at my usual place close to the window.

'The Major has sensational news to tell you.'

Harris gave me a sideways glance, not unlike that of the little robin that waited to be fed of a morning on the window ledge.

'Sensational news?' he repeated, looking at the Major in expectation.

The Major, finding himself the centre of attention, leaned forward in his chair. There was a certain amount of shuffling and, indeed, preening. The yellow cravat was adjusted about his neck. At such times, it was imperative that the narrator is up to the task or else the magic is lost; a good beginning was everything.

I can still recall the events of that morning as though it were yesterday. The Major, being old school, knew well how this game was played. He began his tale at the very beginning and weaved his way steadfastly and at a measured pace through it. His usual short sentences were replaced by much longer ones – perhaps he was under the illusion that such a technique would prolong the telling.

Having the two of us in the palm of his hand, as it were, he slowly played out every word, distributing his largesse like a headmaster at a prize-giving day.

'I was out and about early this morning, walking the dog, and had just turned for home when I spied Brendan, the postman, in the distance. Our paths don't always cross at that time of day but, when they do, we normally wave to each other and continue on our respective ways. But this morning, he held his ground and, sensing something had unsettled him, I walked towards him to investigate his odd behaviour.'

'I enquired if anything was the matter and it was then he spoke to me of the robbery. He told me that a bank in Oughterard was broken into last night and a huge sum of money had been stolen.'

Glancing at Harris, I discerned from his lacklustre attitude that he was quickly losing interest in the story. As if to reinforce my thoughts, he said, 'Surely this robbery is of little consequence? Where is this place – Oughterard?'

'Do you remember when we were on our way back from Louisburgh and you remarked on the name on the signpost?' I said.

'Yes, but where exactly is it located?'

'It's a small village, close to Maam Cross.'

'Maam Cross? Where or what is that?'

'Might I suggest that one of you purchase a map of the west of Ireland; it is surprising how educational it can be,' said the Major, chuckling to himself.

'There is one in the chest of drawers in my bedroom,' I said.

'Excellent! That's the place to keep it hidden and out of sight. What are you two like?'

That put us in our place.

The Major continued: 'This bank in Oughterard was chosen as a collection centre for old bank notes that were being withdrawn from circulation in the counties of Mayo and Galway. It is my understanding that bank notes deteriorate rapidly and are replaced by new ones. This is normal practice, but the logistics of carrying out such a task are daunting.'

Harris reached for his pipe and tobacco pouch and, still looking at the Major, began the ritual of filling it.

'Old bank notes,' he said. 'Now that is very interesting.'

'Yes,' said the Major, 'bank notes are replaced, and we hardly even notice it. I don't know for how long notes remain in circulation, but it must be for several years. Recently, the banking powers decided that certain used notes should be withdrawn from circulation and replaced with new ones.

'During the past few months, every bank throughout the counties of Mayo and Galway has been retaining old notes as they were lodged and storing them in their safes. To facilitate the collection of the notes, it was decided by the banking authorities, in consultation with the powers that be in the Guards, that a central collection point would be set up. It made sense as the logistics of a security lorry calling to every single bank to make the collections would be time-consuming and risky. Better, instead, to have all the banks make their own arrangements to have the money transferred on the same day to one central point.'

I was pleased to notice that, at this juncture, Harris was taking more than a passing interest in the unfolding story. He was now sitting in a more upright position with his head cocked to one side, listening intently. So engrossed was he, that he was absentmindedly searching his pockets for a box of matches, not realising they were sitting on the table in front of him.

I watched his futile search with amusement and wondered if I should point out to him the whereabouts of his combustible friends. I thought about it for a minute and then sat back to watch his antics.

The Major continued. 'Yesterday was the designated day for the notes collected during the past number of weeks to be transferred to Oughterard, and each bank delivered them on a rota basis. Tight security was in place for the mammoth task and everything went to plan. When the final delivery was received, a tally of the collections was undertaken, and every sack of money was accounted for.

'Two security lorries arrived in Oughterard that evening around seven o'clock to collect all the sacks for transportation to a location in Dublin where the notes were to be incinerated. It was at this point, as the sacks were being transferred to the lorries, that the theft was discovered. The extraordinary thing is that no one knows how the money was stolen.'

I could see the intense excitement in Harris' eyes as he listened to the unfolding story.

'Inspector Hennessy is in charge of the investigation.'

Harris nodded his head; I imagined he was thinking that, at some stage, the Inspector would call on him.

I interrupted. 'I'm so sorry, Major, but I forgot all about your tea and scones.'

'Tea and scones? I think the Major would prefer a glass of Jameson,' Harris remarked.

The Major winced at the mention of the whiskey and took a deep breath. He wrestled with the choice of fare offered and then said, 'I think it is a bit late in the morning for tea and scones, I will take a whiskey.'

I could only smile at this remarkable logic so eloquently expounded by him.

# CHAPTER 3

The improvement in Harris was significant and on Saturday morning, the day following the Major's visit, I was surprised and pleased when he suggested we go for a brisk walk to Mannane. He was a changed person as we discussed the story that had been recounted the previous day. The pale February sun was sweeping the landscape as we trudged along the road we travelled so often. The bitter cold that had lingered for months had eased and a gradual change was taking place. The mornings were now much brighter and the presence of spring was apparent on the mossy banks of the roadside on which tiny coloured flowers were beginning to peep out.

Sedgewick Harris was much taken by the events at Oughterard. The lack of information on these happenings was frustrating, but trying to work out what had taken place was helping his recovery. Our walk towards the village was uneventful but pleasant, and we strode along, both of us engrossed in our own little world. It is not always necessary to converse in such circumstances and therein lies the secret of good conversation.

We had hardly advanced a half mile when the tranquility of the countryside was disturbed by the noise of an approaching car. The sound intensified as it drew closer and, suddenly, a black car rounded the bend, travelling at speed.

'Inspector Hennessy!' said Harris.

The alacrity with which he recognised the car registered immediately with me and I realised he had been watching for it.

The car ground to a halt and Hennessy opened a side window. 'Get in!' he shouted above the noise of the engine.

We climbed in and he drove back to the cottage. Once inside, we took up our positions in the front room, close to the turf fire. It was burning brightly for I had stacked it with sods of turf less than a half hour previously, before we'd left for our walk.

'I'm sure you have heard of the bank robbery at Oughterard?'

'Yes, Major Jones came by yesterday morning and gave a brief outline of the astonishing events,' replied Harris.

'Ah, the irascible Major,' said the Inspector, 'forever poking his nose into all the goings-on in the district.'

'He is a kind and generous man,' I exclaimed, rushing to his defence.

'Indeed, but he has this knack of turning up at every event that occurs, no matter how insignificant.'

'That is understandable,' said Harris. 'In this quiet backwater, very little happens and when it does, it assumes an exaggerated importance, way out of all proportion. We are all attracted to those little events that bring a bit of excitement and colour to our day. The recent goings-on in a small bank in the middle of Connemara, whilst newsworthy and of significance, as explained by the Major, can scarcely be that important.'

Hennessy stared at Harris for what seemed an eternity and then slowly and deliberately delivered the coup de grace.

'I don't know how many banks there are in the counties of Galway and Mayo but, at a guess, I would say a few hundred. This morning I received confirmation of the final amount of money transferred to Oughterard.'

He paused and looked at Harris and then over at me, not unlike a magician who waits for the drum roll to finish before producing the rabbit from the hat. We both waited in keen anticipation.

'The amount of money transferred into the bank at Oughterard the day before yesterday was just in excess of a £300,000.'

Harris sat bolt upright in his armchair at the mention of the figure and I began to calculate the number of Morris Minors at £475 each I could purchase with such a sum.

'You are aware that this money was destined for an incinerator and, as such, had already been taken out of circulation. The amount stolen is still legal tender. Even though the banks were collecting old notes for the past month or more, there would be a vast quantity of them still in circulation. Whoever stole the notes will have no difficulty passing them on. There is no record of the serial numbers.'

The Inspector continued: 'I know how interested you are in matters of this nature and while I am confident I will soon arrest the thieves, I decided to drop in on you on my way back from headquarters in Galway. You and Jonathan have been helpful in recent cases.'

Helpful? A slight understatement, I thought, but let it go. Harris, I knew, wasn't bothered; to him it was all a game.

Hennessy reached inside his brown sports jacket, withdrew a small notebook, and consulted it before continuing his narrative.

'The bank is situated at the end of the main street and is one in a terrace of five houses that were built over fifty years ago. Initially, these were private dwelling houses but, over the years, the usage changed in all but one of them. The first premises in the terrace is a newsagents; a solicitor, Ivor Nugent, lives in the next house and runs his legal practice from it. Then there is the bank and next to it a betting shop. A young family lives in the end house.'

'I don't understand how a small bank could be capable of housing so much money. It scarcely seems possible,' remarked a mystified Harris.

'It was one of the first things to enter my head on hearing the news,' replied the Inspector. 'However, it soon became clear why this particular bank was chosen.'

'When the decision was made by the directors of the bank to withdraw the old notes, it was immediately notified to senior officials at the Guards' headquarters. Both parties held a few meetings and following from that a strategy was devised that would be low key and effective. Oughterard was chosen because it was a small village that could be easily protected while the transfers were taking place. There was no bank in the west of Ireland that had a big enough safe capable of holding the number of sacks of cash that needed to be stored during the operation. The solution to this problem lay in the bank at Oughterard.'

'Really?' I asked, surprised at this statement.

'The bank is a medium-sized building,' continued the Inspector, 'and three people are employed there – a manager, a bank teller and a secretary. It is not busy as there are not sufficient people in the village or surrounding area availing of its services. The banking business takes place on the left-hand side as you enter the narrow front door while across the corridor the entire right-hand side consists of one very big, empty room. The decision was taken to use this room as the temporary storage area for the bank notes. Effectively, it would serve as a safe. It had the advantage of being easily protected by members of the Guards who were positioned inside and outside the bank at all times, from the moment the operation was put into place. There was ample space to store the hundreds of sacks when they arrived from all over Mayo and Galway.'

'That makes sense,' remarked Harris, cleaning the debris from his pipe.

'Six weeks ago, instructions were given to all the banks managers in the two counties to instruct their staff to commence withdrawing old bank notes as they were presented by customers. Special sacks were issued to the banks in which to place the notes. They came in five different colours – red for ten shilling notes, white for £1 notes, blue for £5 notes, green for £10 notes, and yellow for £20 notes.

'The whereabouts of the selected storage place at Oughterard was known to very few people and the banks involved were only informed of the location the day before they were to deliver the money they had gathered during the six-week period. Everyone associated with the cash transfers is adamant that everything went according to plan and, as I've already said, all the sacks delivered were accounted for at the end of the day.'

'That seems pretty clear-cut,' I suggested.

'Yes, Jonathan, the difficult logistical problem ran smoothly and the sacks were locked securely in the bank before six o'clock on Thursday evening, awaiting the arrival of the collection lorries. Two large security lorries arrived in Oughterard around eight o'clock that evening and the task of loading the sacks commenced immediately. A number of floodlights had been erected outside the bank to facilitate the loading. The area around the bank was closed to the villagers and traffic was diverted away from it.

'The transferring of the sacks to the lorries from the big room went smoothly and by ten o'clock they were halfway through their task. After a short break, work recommenced and steady progress was made. It was coming up to midnight and there were less than fifty sacks remaining lying against the end wall when a truly staggering sight was revealed. As the security men began moving those final sacks, they discovered a large hole, at least four feet square, in the wall. Someone had broken into the bank room from the premises next door.'

The effect of these words on Harris was almost electric. He rubbed his hands in unmitigated delight. 'How innovative, how clever!' he commented.

'For the life of me, I don't see what you find amusing,' said a peeved Hennessy. 'This is a most serious matter.'

'Please forgive my unwarranted outburst, but one has to admire the ingenuity of the daring robbers.'

'It was a well-planned robbery but I have no admiration for these sort of people,' replied the still-irked Inspector.

There followed a silence while Hennessy took a packet of Players from his pocket and set about lighting a cigarette. He inhaled deeply and then blew the smoke upwards to the ceiling. All I needed now was for Harris to light his pipe. I shuddered at the thoughts of the dense fog that would ensue if that happened. Luckily, it did not.

'I was thinking,' said Hennessy, 'if you have the time, yourself and Jonathan might accompany me to Oughterard to see the scene of the robbery. I am on my way over there now. Does that suit you?'

'Yes,' replied Harris, 'we can go straight away. Is that okay with you, Jonathan?'

There was no necessity for him to ask; I was eager to have a look at that bank as soon as possible.

\*\*\*

The car journey took us through the most beautiful countryside imaginable. Onwards through many tiny villages we went, in and out of places and districts with magical sounding names. We drove through Recess and, much to the delight of Harris, we came to Maam Cross.

'This is all so wonderful,' he murmured with sincerity in his voice.

We were approaching Oughterard when Harris asked, 'Was the break-in made from the office of the solicitor?'

'Yes, it was, but why did you think that?' replied Hennessy.

'Nothing, just something that crossed my mind.'

I wondered to myself what the something was that had crossed that weird mind of his.

Hennessy parked the car in an alleyway off the main street and we walked with him to the front of the building. Having entered the bank, we followed him down a short corridor and made our way to the big room where the break-in had occurred. It was a forlorn, desolate-looking place, stark and empty.

Directly in front of us was a wall with a large hole in it. The Inspector ducked his head and walked through the hole into the solicitor's office next door. We followed and entered a small room that was covered with broken stones and plaster. The debris from the wall was scattered all over the floor, as were a number of unopened, coloured sacks. On one side, old legal files were stacked high, covered in dust and pieces of stone.

Harris immediately set to work examining the scene. I was content to stare at the large hole in the wall, wondering who the ingenious person was that had masterminded this remarkable robbery. Harris had gone unusually quiet and even though he was standing next to me, his concentration was elsewhere. He was staring up at the ceiling and I noticed the frown on his forehead. Suddenly, he walked into the adjacent kitchen and returned with a chair. He placed it close to the wall and stood upon it. His tilted head was some inches from the ceiling and he was looking intently at it.

'What is it, Harris? Have you found something?'

'Yes, a small hole has been bored into the wall just below the ceiling.'

'Why would the thieves do that?'

He did not respond but just climbed down from the chair, muttering to himself. Once more, he picked up the chair and proceeded to walk with it through the large hole in the wall back into the bank room next door. I followed him, determined not to miss anything. He placed the chair against the wall and climbed on to it. If the small hole that had been bored in the wall on other side had come all the way through, then he would have been looking directly into it. From my position, I could see that there was no mark of any sort on the wall.

But he was not finished yet, and I watched in astonishment as he produced a large magnifying glass from his coat pocket. He placed it close to his right eye and began a detailed inspection of the wall.

There was a funny side to all this and I just could not help myself: 'Would you like me to get you a deerstalker hat and a Sherlock Holmes pipe?' I asked, teasingly.

'Very amusing, Jonathan,' Harris replied.

He climbed down from the chair and returned the magnifying glass to his pocket.

'How did you know there was a hole up there, under the ceiling?' I asked.

'Where else would it be,' he replied dismissively.

He returned the chair to the kitchen, came back out, and stood beside me in the room. He was pensive but alert, his eyes darting around, looking everywhere for something that he obviously expected to find.

'Can I help you? What are you looking for?'

'I'm looking for a …' the sentence trailed off and he got down on his hands and knees and retrieved a brown ruler from under a table. It was an everyday type of instrument, twelve inches in length. He looked closely at it and nodded his head in a knowing way.

'Just as I thought,' he said.

I was at a loss to understand what exactly was going on. I was standing in the centre of the room, surrounded on the one side by old files that were stacked against a wall, while all about me numerous coloured sacks lay unopened and scattered on the wooden floor among the debris.

'The thieves must have been disturbed,' I said, pointing to the sacks.

He looked at me and replied, 'I don't think they were disturbed. Do you notice anything peculiar about the sacks?'

'They are still full of cash.'

'That is true, Jonathan, but look at the colours.'

'What you mean? Hennessy has already explained all that to us.'

'There are at least fifty sacks full of money lying on the floor but not one of them is coloured green or yellow. The Inspector told us that the £10 notes were in green sacks and the £20 notes in yellow ones? The thieves knew the colour of the sacks they were looking for. How could they have known that?'

I had no idea but, so as not to let myself down in front of him, I nodded my head in a serious manner and even stroked my chin contemplatively.

'We are dealing with an astute protagonist who grasped the significance of the different colours. He worked it out very quickly and gave instructions to the others to take the green and yellow sacks only. Credit to him for being so perceptive.'

# CHAPTER 4

We were in the small storage room when Hennessy came back. He was smoking one of his infernal cigarettes and looking at his notebook.

'I'm off now. I'm wanted in Galway but Sergeant Wallace will drive you back to Mannane when you have finished here. The initial entry was through the kitchen window; you will see it when you go in there. I'll keep in touch.'

The kitchen was a mess with dirty dishes and cups and saucers stacked on the table and in the small sink. A half-used packet of butter was lying open on the table along with partially used loaves of bread. An ashtray filled with cigarette stubs complemented the dire setting. There were four chairs haphazardly arranged around the table, giving the impression that the bank robbers had been sitting there and suddenly decided to get up and take off. Broken glass lay on the floor, directly under the window, where the thieves had broken in.

One of them had broken a hole in the window and reached their hand through and undone the clasp, pushed open the window, and stepped inside to the kitchen. The back door was then opened to allow the rest of the gang to enter carrying the tools that were used to break through the wall.

Harris walked around the kitchen for a short while; then he went out to the small back garden and examined the broken window from there. He was pensive as he stared into the distance.

'I just wonder,' he said when he came back in.

'Why do you just wonder?' I enquired politely.

'Indeed,' he replied, 'that is a good question.'

I wondered why I even bothered to ask questions.

\*\*\*

We left the kitchen and made our way to a short corridor on which three doors were located. Harris opened the first door and we entered a room that was furnished with a few armchairs and a small table. He glanced around and walked out again. The next room was a very plain office with a telephone on the desk and a few writing pads. We then entered the third room; it was much smaller than the other two and was obviously used by the solicitor's secretary. Once more, Harris showed little interest and, nodding his head, he walked out.

'Let's have a look upstairs,' he said.

Nugent lived alone and slept in the room that was to the front of the house and which looked down on to the street. It gave a side view to the entrance to the bank. The bedroom had a decent bed and adequate furniture, but the other two rooms had no beds and little else. Obviously, they were never used.

'I would like to know a bit more about this solicitor, Ivor Nugent. Hennessy barely mentioned him, which is most peculiar. We will just have to wait until the Inspector makes contact with us again.'

It was time to return to Mannane so we went outside and found Sergeant Wallace who drove us back to my house.

\*\*\*

Later that afternoon, a very tired looking Inspector arrived at the cottage. It was evident he was under extreme pressure and I think he was glad to be able to call on us.

'The top brass in Dublin expect me to work miracles. They appear to think that I should have apprehended the thieves by now.'

Harris was very sympathetic. 'Inspector,' he said, 'you will always get harassment from the people above you and the clever thing to do is to not let it get to you. I have always approached each case I become involved in as a game and am even open-minded enough to consider defeat.'

'And have you ever been defeated?' I asked, astonished.

'No, Jonathan, although in the case of the Missing Cricket Umpire all seemed lost. Then, I accidentally stumbled on the solution. That book contained seventy-two pages and, but for a remark by the green grocer's assistant, I would have missed that obvious clue.'

'Of course you would,' I said, completely baffled or, should I say, stumped.

Hennessy was looking at Harris in wonderment.

'Perhaps a glass of Jameson would be an ideal tonic at this time,' I suggested.

In a matter of minutes we were seated, fortified by the whiskey and warmed by the heat of the blazing turf fire.

Hennessy spoke. 'You have inspected the solicitor's house and office and seen where the break-in was made? It would have taken many hours to chisel through that stone wall and the work could only be undertaken while the bank was closed and the staff had gone home for the night. The bank manager told me that the staff arrive at nine o'clock each morning and depart at 5.30 p.m. The manager, who lives some five miles away, comes in each morning at eight o'clock and usually goes home at the same time as the staff. The bank is closed on Saturdays and Sundays.'

'Where was the solicitor when all this was taking place?' asked Harris. 'I assume he was away somewhere otherwise you would have arrested him.'

The Inspector, who, at this point, was consulting his notebook, looked up and said, 'The solicitor left Oughterard last Friday morning, a full week before the robbery. He went on a fishing trip to Finlough, a lake close to the village of Leenane. It is about twenty miles from Oughterard. He was absent for the full week and his office was closed all that time.'

'How convenient,' said Harris.

'In fairness, he is a fishing fanatic and every so often goes to this old, rundown fishing hut near the shores of the Finlough, across the road from the old Delphi Lodge estate.'

'Have you spoken to him since the robbery?' asked Harris.

'As soon as the break-in was discovered, instructions were given to locate Nugent. He was our prime suspect and orders were issued to apprehend him immediately. Two local Guards from Leenane went to Finlough and located him at the fishing lodge. They brought him back to the Guards' barracks at Oughterard where he was detained overnight.

'In the morning, I arrived at the barracks and took a statement from him concerning his movements over the past number of days. He was then brought to his office to assist with the enquiries. The front door to the office was locked when we arrived, just as he had left it seven days previously when he went fishing, and he opened it with his key. I accompanied him around the house and we checked all the rooms. Nugent was shocked by the state of the storage room. But you have seen all that yourself. Did you notice all the sacks still full of cash lying about the floor? The thieves must have left in a hurry.'

'Indeed,' replied Harris.

Feeling somewhat excluded from the conversation, I asked, 'Was there anything unusual or out of place on the premises?'

Harris looked intently at the Inspector.

'There was something,' answered Hennessy. 'The small kitchen had been used to make tea and sandwiches. A cursory examination of that area indicated that at least three people had been there.'

Now feeling very confident, I asked another question, 'How did you come to the conclusion that there were three people?'

'There were three dirty mugs on the table and quite a number of partially used loaves of bread, as well as butter and jam. Nugent told me that the kitchen table was clean when he had left to go fishing and that the bread and butter were not the sort used by him. '

'Interesting,' muttered Harris.

'However, the really unusual thing was the ashtray. It was crammed full of cigarette stubs and, on closer examination, I made out three different brands.'

'I'm impressed,' said a smiling Harris. 'There is hope for you yet, Inspector.'

Hennessy ignored the comment and continued to speak, every now and then consulting the notebook in his hand.

'From all accounts, this Nugent fellow is a splendid chap. He is in his early forties, full of energy, unmarried and, I would imagine, fond of the good life. He drives a distinctive two-seater red sports car. Very flashy, I'm told.'

For some reason, I immediately thought of the beat-up Morris Minor that the Major had loaned me and of the difficulty I was having trying to drive it.

Hennessy took a sip of his whiskey and continued. 'He likes to sneak off every now and then and fish along the shores of the lake on his own. The old hut at the lakeside is pretty basic and the accommodation is spartan. I'm not even sure if it is connected to the electricity network.'

'Have you been there?' enquired Harris.

'I was there a long time ago for some reason or other, but not in recent times.'

Harris said nothing but he had that faraway look I had come to recognise. Was he on to something? What was it the Inspector had said that had caused this reaction?

'I presume Nugent is your prime suspect?' said Harris.

'Yes, my suspicions immediately were on him. Even though he was away fishing, there was nothing to prevent him driving back to his house late each evening when everyplace was deserted. He could get to work on the wall and then, early in the morning, before anyone was about, drive back to the lakeside.'

'Why have you not arrested him?' Harris asked.

'Enquiries in the Leenane area and in and about Finlough established that he had been fishing there all the time and was seen by several people during the week. He could have driven back to Oughterard each evening; it is only twenty-three miles distant, spent a few hours working on the wall, and returned early in the morning to the lake. But he is an intelligent man and would realise someone would see him on the road.'

'That red sports car would easily be spotted,' I pointed out, once more getting into the conversation.

'There is one other interesting thing,' said the inspector.

Harris and I, in unison – or so it seemed – immediately sat up in our chairs and took notice.

'A circus arrived in the area ten days ago. They have set up in a field on the edge of Oughterard; a bit of a coincidence?'

# CHAPTER 5

The following morning, Harris insisted on going to Finlough to visit the fishing hut. I was wary of driving the Major's car on such a long journey but knew that it would be an opportunity for me to work on my driving skills. I drove carefully and it was a relief when I saw the signpost indicating the turn-off for Leenane. We stopped at the first house we came upon and I went in to ask for directions.

'Is that the solicitor fellow who scoots around in the red racing car?' the occupant of the house asked.

'Yes, the very man,' I replied.

'Saw him fishing at the Horseshoe Pool, down by the stream near the lake, during the past few days. Bit odd.'

'Really? Can you direct me to the place he was fishing? I'm hoping he is still there as I need to speak to him.'

The directions were excellent and within ten minutes I was parking the car in front of the small, dilapidated stone hut. I could tell that, in another age, it must have been a splendid place. Much of the timber facade had succumbed to the elements and it was surrounded by a small forest that, over the years, had quietly sneaked up on it and now almost hid it fully from view.

Looking up along the Delphi Valley with its lakes and tiny islands and small streams that travel from far away, I was reminded of the words of Tennyson:

*Willows whiten, aspens shiver,*

*The sunbeam showers break and quiver*

*In the stream that runneth ever*

*By the island in the river.*

'How apt, Jonathan, you have that capacity to bring out the dreamer in me.'

Leaving the car in the small clearing in front of the hut, I followed Harris who was heading for the lake shore. However, his long strides covered the ground quickly so I decided to remain where I was until he returned. I could see him in the distance, head bent low, examining the ground, his hands thrust deep into his overcoat pockets. He had difficulty making progress as some of the trees had moved away from the forest over the years, and a few of them had even fallen into the lake.

Soon he was back, talking to himself. As he passed me, he raised his voice and said, 'There is nothing here on the lakeside for us to see. I think we should go into Leenane and see if we can get something to eat.'

\*\*\*

I drove to the village and parked the car outside the Leenane Hotel, an imposing place overlooking Killary Harbour. Harris was much taken by the breathtaking views and lingered for a while, looking into the distance across the simmering sea. Tea and sandwiches were quickly provided, and it was only then I realised how hungry I was.

Harris had deserted me and I could see him in the distance, speaking to someone. When he returned, he said, 'It will be dark in a few hours, but I have just one more call to make on the other side of the village.'

Seeing my perplexed expression, he said, 'I enquired from the proprietor if the postman lived nearby. He lives out the road and I would like to ask him a few questions. In a small townland, the postman sees everything.'

\*\*\*

We went out the village and Harris told me to stop next to a whitewashed cottage, on an elevated position back from the road. As soon as he knocked on the door, it was opened by a small, pleasant man dressed in a postman's uniform. The buttons of his tunic were undone, an indication that his work for the day was over.

Harris did all the talking and, to my surprise, indicated that we were intent on joining a friend of ours who was staying at a fishing lodge. 'We called there, and the place is deserted and there is no sign of our colleague. The hotel proprietor gave me your address and said you might be able to assist me. Did you happen to notice anyone down by the lake during the past few days?'

The postman scratched his rather big nose and replied in a lilting voice, 'I see everything that goes on about here. My route takes me past the old fishing hut down by the lake, but I rarely have any letters or parcels to deliver there anymore. It's not like the old days when it was occupied for most of the year and scarcely a day went by that I did not cycle down there.'

'Indeed,' said Harris politely. 'Was there any activity at the hut or the lake in the past week or two?'

'The solicitor fellow, Nugent, was there fishing. You will not catch much at this time of the year. He came on Friday of last week. I saw the little sports car parked there when I cycled along the top road.'

'Don't tell me he was there the whole week and we come along today and miss him,' replied Harris.

'He was there all week. I saw him in the village on Saturday, or maybe it was Friday of last week. He walked past my gate as I was coming out and headed out the road.'

'Thank you so much for your time. You have been most helpful,' Harris said.

*** 

As we drove back through the village, he said, 'Would you mind returning to the hut? I would like to have another look at it.'

Back at the fishing hut, I once again stopped the car in the clearing and we walked towards the small front door. It was locked and we didn't have a key. There were small windows on either side of the door and we pressed our faces to each of them and had a good look inside.

In my mind, I had imagined a cosy little hideaway, full of nooks and crannies. What I was looking at, however, was a bleak, stark room at the far side of which was a large, open fireplace, similar to those used in farmhouse kitchens. It was filled with debris from an old bird's nest that had fallen down the chimney some time ago. Stacked on either side of the fireplace were neatly arranged rows of turf. A cot bed had been placed beside the wall to the left of the fireplace and a few dirty blankets had been thrown on it. It made a depressing sight. Further along, to the other side of the fireplace, were two chairs and a small, simple, wooden table. There was little else in the way of furniture except for more rows of turf leaning against the wall.

'This is disappointing,' said Harris. 'There is nothing of interest here.'

We walked around to the back of the building and there was nothing there except a large reek of turf. It would have been put there in early September and built in such a way that the outer sods of turf would act as a shelter for those inside. The reek was built in layers, sod upon sod, and was about ten feet long, four feet high, and four feet wide. It was a wonderful feat of workmanship. A large tarpaulin had been thrown over it, but it had slipped and was now barely covering the turf.

'What do you think, Harris? Splendid piece of workmanship.'

'Indeed,' he replied.

***

It was an unusually dull evening, typical of the grey, overcast weather that lurks about the tiny fields and hedges of Connemara at this time of year. We drove away from the fishing lodge and headed in the direction of Ballyconneely. It soon became obvious that resort would have to be made to the use of the car headlights. This would be a tricky operation as, not having driven in the dark before, and being confused by the knobs and dials on display in front of me, I was unsure how to go about turning them on.

I pressed various switches and managed to get the windscreen wipers working, as well as putting on an overhead light. I pressed a few more buttons and nothing, to my knowledge happened. Maybe the side lights had come on, but I didn't think so. There was only one thing for it – Harris would have to get out and look at the front of the car and let me know if the lights were working. He was reluctant to get out, but he did.

We often look back at things that occur in our lifetime and have a good laugh. Hindsight is wonderful. I got confused; that's what happened. It was never my intention to press the accelerator, it was a pure accident. These things happen.

Harris, shivering with the cold, was looking intently at the front of the car when it lurched forward at a fair speed. There was nothing I could do; the car seemed to take on a life of its own. Harris, instead of retreating, as a normal person would do, advanced at some pace and launched himself onto the bonnet of the car.

His large nose was pressed against the windscreen and there was a wild stare in the only eye visible to me. His lips were frantically moving but I could not hear a word he was saying. He was mouthing something, over and over. It sounded like, 'The brakes! The brakes!' Of course, in the upheaval, I had overlooked the fact that the car was in motion. Not at a great speed, for I am a careful driver, but then, I suppose, if one is hanging onto the bonnet of a car for dear life even the slowest speed is potentially dangerous!

Instantly, I slammed on the brakes and the car stopped abruptly. Harris, like a pilot in combat whose plane has taken a direct hit, was ejected from the bonnet and sailed swiftly, if in an ungainly manner, over a low stone wall. I rushed from the driver's seat and ran towards the spot where I had the last sighting of him.

'Harris! Harris! Are you alright?' I cried, frantically. There followed a low moan and a muffled call of anguish.

'It's my ankle! It's twisted and either broken or sprained.'

I jumped over the low wall and knelt down next to him. I carefully assisted him to his feet, guided him through a gap in the wall, and got him back to the car. He was moaning quite a bit. It was then that I noticed the car headlights were on; things were looking up. We drove home in silence, save for the odd moan and inaudible muttering from Harris who was slumped across the back seat.

*\*\*\**

There is no doubt but that Miss Noonan, the housekeeper, was a treasure. As soon as the car pulled up at the cottage, she came out to welcome me and especially Harris, to whom she had taken a shine from the very first day she'd met him. She was still in the process of getting to know him and was a bit in awe when in his presence.

'I'm delighted to see you again,' she said.

For a moment, I thought she was going to courtesy.

'It's always so nice to meet you,' he replied.

'Come in, come in, I have a lovely pot of Irish stew ready for both of you.'

Harris limped towards the door and Miss Noonan stepped to one side so he could pass by. She watched him closely and whispered loudly to me, 'He is so distinguished looking, especially with the limp. Has he had it long?'

'Twenty minutes, my good lady, twenty minutes!' came Harris' high-pitched voice from inside the cottage.

The Irish stew and the glass of Jameson gently eased my friend into a more placid state of mind. Every now and then he would look at me and shake his head. We had barely spoken which, maybe, was a good thing. There is a time for silence. I could see he was coming round, but would require more coaxing. The second glass had the desired effect.

'You know, Jonathan, only that you drive at the speed of a snail I might have been killed.'

I was well able for him. 'You should be thankful to me for saving your life.'

'What do you mean *saving my life?* You almost killed me.'

'But you just implied that you might have been killed had I been driving faster. You can't have it every way. Do you not agree? The least you could do is say thanks.'

That threw him. He was at a loss to know how he might respond to my ridiculous logic. Then a broad smile lit up his face, a sort of magic appeared around his features, and he was the old Harris once again.

'I could never fall out with you, Jonathan.'

'The feeling is mutual.'

# CHAPTER 6

It was lunchtime after our visit to the fishing hut at Finlough close to the Delphi Lodge estate and

Harris was agitated. I had come to know his methods very well and could see that he was striving desperately to make sense of the facts that had been assembled over the last few days.

'You know, Jonathan, I have all the relevant information required and yet I'm no further on in finding a solution. Something is missing.'

'Well,' I replied mischievously, 'you can't have all the information if something is missing.'

He smiled and nodded his head, 'Very droll, Jonathan, but the solution must be staring me in the face and yet I can't see it.'

I knew by the way this conversation was going that Harris was about to fall back on a method I had so often seen him use back in the college days. He would speak in a rhetorical manner and, using this technique, allow his thought processes to be aired publicly without interruption. This gave him an opportunity to speak out loud and arrange, in a flawless and precise manner, the numerous segments of information revolving through his brilliant mind. It was an essential and important part of the display about to take place that the briar pipe was primed and going at full steam.

Just as I predicted, he rose from the armchair and, pacing the room, began to speak in a clear, loud voice.

'My immediate inclination was to suspect Nugent, the solicitor. As the Inspector has already indicated, what was to prevent him driving back from the fishing lodge and lying low in his office for the week? You will recall the rather large, enclosed garden that backed onto the rear of the house when we were walking through the kitchen?'

At this juncture, it is necessary to understand that all questions asked in the midst of this preamble are rhetorical. I had not paid any particular attention to the back garden and, as a response from me was not expected, it did not matter one way or the other.

'It would have been easy for Nugent to park the car in the back garden and leave it there for the week. The difficulty was getting the car in there without being observed. But once it was there, no one could see over the high wall from the road into the garden. Maybe that is what he did. You noticed how enclosed the garden was and the large double door that gave access to it from the back laneway?'

As no answer was expected, there was no requirement to display my ignorance, but, once again, I marvelled at his attention to detail. Nothing escaped his notice. He continued to pace the room.

'People in the village would have been known that Nugent had gone fishing. If someone had seen him returning to Oughterard, they would not have paid much notice to it. They would assume he had come back to collect something he had forgotten and had returned to the lodge later.

'Hennessy told us that Nugent went to the lodge on the Friday morning, a full week before the delivery of the bank notes. The postman also verified that he saw him fishing on the lake. So, if Nugent was at the fishing lodge from that Friday onwards, then the house was unoccupied for almost a week before the robbery. The thieves would have had all day Saturday and Sunday to work on the wall as the bank was closed. On the weekdays, they would have worked after the bank had closed and before it opened the following morning.'

'Do you mind if I stop you there to ask a question?'

'By all means, please do.'

'How could the thieves have known that the sacks of money were about to be delivered to the bank in Oughterard? Was it not meant to be a secret?'

'I am not yet certain, Jonathan, how the thieves found this out but, regardless of that, I must carry on. In the past, whilst engaged on other cases, I have discovered that as an investigation progresses, things begin to fall into place. I am certain that, in due course, the answer to your question will be revealed. What matters now is to find the money and, with it, the thieves. You will recall that Inspector Hennessy told us that the Guards in Leenane arrested Nugent at the lodge just hours after the break-in was discovered. At this point, I was still uncertain if he had played any part in the robbery and that is the reason we went to Finlough yesterday. The positive identification of Nugent by the postman placed him away from the scene of the crime during the last number of days and so I have discounted him as a suspect.'

I felt I had to say my piece. 'Despite what everyone says, I still think he could have driven back each night and returned to Finlough the next morning.'

'I am inclined to agree with you, but when the Guards arrested him a few hours after the robbery he was in the fishing lodge and the postman has also given him a tight alibi. The small sports car he drives is well known in these parts and is easily recognisable. Even the man who gave us directions to the lodge yesterday said he saw him fishing along the stream near the lake. He could not have risked driving back and forth as someone would have seen the car. There was no other way for him to get from Finlough to Oughterard except by car. I must admit, Jonathan, that I am no further on in solving this part of the mystery. If Nugent is not the mastermind behind the robbery, then who is?'

'Could it have been someone from the circus?' I suggested, once again interrupting his steady flow of conversation.

'No. Inspector Hennessy and a few of his men will have already called to the circus and checked it out. We would have heard by now if the circus people were involved in the robbery. We may forget about them.'

'Yet someone was in the solicitor's office after Nugent went to the fishing hut last Friday,' I replied.

At this point, Harris sat down and began the laborious task of cleaning his briar pipe. It was an indication that he was in conversation mode and that the time of rhetorical speaking had passed.

'Certainly, someone was there. Can you imagine how many hours of painstaking work was involved in slowly and quietly boring through that stone wall? The row of houses were built in the last century and constructed with hard stone which made the task even more difficult. We have to assume that the thieves broke into the premises on Friday evening, some hours after Nugent had departed for Finlough. They would have been watching for him to leave. Perhaps they were seating in a parked car, observing the office and house.

'The task of breaking through the thick stone wall would have been tedious, and constant care had to be taken that the noise they were making was not heard by passers-by in the street. They would have stuck diligently to their task until they had almost made the breakthrough on the other side. Great care had to be taken that the wall remained intact and was not pierced by the tools they were using.

'Even the smallest particle of mortar falling from the wall onto the floor would have been a disaster,' I said, 'and the Guards and security men, when they came on duty prior to the first sacks being delivered, would have seen this and raised the alarm.'

'Quite so, and that is the reason the smaller hole was bored close to the ceiling.'

'I don't follow your reasoning, Harris.'

'The thieves had to measure how far they could bore through the wall without disturbing the wallpaper on the other side. By boring the small hole, they were able to gradually inch their way forward through the wall. When I looked through that hole, I was able to see the back of the wallpaper and it appeared not to have been disturbed. I even went around, to the bank room and, much to your amusement, used my magnifying glass to confirm that fact.'

'But why did they not bore the small hole near the centre of the wall? It would have been much easier.'

'People, in general, observe things at eye level. They rarely look upwards, and had the wallpaper been pierced near the ceiling, it might not have been noticed, whereas a mark on the wallpaper near the centre of the wall, no matter how small, might have been seen by the Guards and security men. In the case of the Chiming Clock, no one thought to look up at the ceiling – they stared at the clock instead.'

'And was it important to look up?'

'Vital, otherwise that rogue, Winston, would have made off with the priceless Indian sapphire.'

'And you looked up?'

'Of course, it was the natural thing to do.'

Of course, it was, I thought to myself. Why did I even ask?

'The wooden ruler I found under a chair not only measured the distance they had progressed when boring the hole under the ceiling but was used as a sort of sounding board. They would insert the ruler into the small opening they were making and tap it against the rock. From the sound, they could roughly estimate if they were close to breaking through on the other side. It would have been painstaking, meticulous work and they had to be careful as they inched ever closer to touching the back of the wallpaper. Once they were certain they had reached the breakthrough point, they measured the distance with the ruler. Now they could confidently set about making the big breakthrough, knowing the exact distance they had to bore.'

'You have to admire their attention to detail,' I said.

'I'm sure you noticed the thick wallpaper; it is a type used on cracked and damaged walls. It is strong and durable and does not tear easily. That made the task easier.'

Of course I had not noticed the wallpaper, but I was not about to admit that.

'A deep blue colour, if I remember correctly,' I commented.

'White, with a red rose through it,' he replied.

Why couldn't I keep my mouth shut?

'From an upstairs window, the thieves observed the sacks being delivered and knew when it was opportune to break through the final bit of the wall. They made an educated guess that the sacks would have been placed against the walls as they were put in the room. It would be the natural thing to do. They counted the sacks as they were taken in and perhaps after a hundred or so were delivered, they calculated that the wall, backing on the solicitor's office, was almost covered by that stage.'

'They carefully broke through the final bit of the wall and made sure their assumptions were correct. Once they saw the sacks, they began pulling them out as quickly as they could.'

'There is something that strikes me as odd.'

'And what is that, Jonathan?'

'How did the thieves know that Nugent would be away fishing last week?'

'I asked the Inspector that very question, and he told me a notice was pinned on the front door of his office for the last few weeks, alerting people to this. He had even put an advertisement in the local newspaper.'

'But how could the thieves know all this money was being transferred to Oughterard on last Thursday?'

'I don't have an answer.'

'You don't have an answer?'

'No.'

'Oh.'

'Don't sound so surprised. There are times when even I do not have the answer to something.'

'Oh.'

'Regardless of the answer to your question, they somehow found out about the plans for moving the money. Lack of information should never hider the progress of an investigation. As a case gathers momentum, matters that were puzzling fall into place and the logical order is restored. At this juncture, they have the bank notes and the prime objective is to locate that money. I am convinced the stolen sacks are hidden somewhere nearby. The entire country is almost at a standstill with the roadblocks that have been put in place. The thieves cannot risk moving the sacks of cash. The money is not too far away.'

\*\*\*

The lazy afternoon began to drag a bit, and Harris was again pacing the room. All the facts he had accumulated were whirring around in that weird brain of his. Looking out the window, I watched a pair of starlings swooping about the cottage. They would fly in under the eaves, settle for a while, and then take off again. Within minutes, they would be back again for another look. I was fascinated by them.

'Why are you staring out the window with a smile on your face?' Harris asked.

'It's the starlings. They are searching for a place in the eaves of the cottage to build a nest. The locals say it is a sign of a good summer when they begin nesting so early in the year.'

'Indeed,' he said, still deep in thought.

There had been a gradual drop in the temperature throughout the afternoon and it was essential to keep the fire blazing.

'It is going to be a very cold night. I am going out to bring some more turf in before it gets dark.'

I had no sooner said these words than Harris stopped in his tracks and, in a raised, excited voice, said, 'Of course that's it – the starlings and the turf fire!'

'I am lost. What are you going on about?'

'Quick! We must get back to the lake lodge. We might yet be in time.'

'But, Harris, it will be dark in a few hours.'

'All the more reason to hurry.'

\*\*\*

I had grown in confidence with my driving and set off at a good speed for Finlough. As it happened, Major Jones was standing outside his front gate talking to someone when we went flashing past in his car. Such was our speed that he was almost blown off the road. I looked in the rear-view mirror and could see him shaking his fist at me.

Why were we returning to Finlough? I was completely at a loss at this sudden turn of events, but as my concentration was now on keeping the car between the hedges on either side of the road, I had no time to question the reasons for this abrupt departure to the lodge. There was no conversation but every now and then Harris would mutter words like, 'stupid', 'idiot', 'imbecile'.' 'Idiot' was repeated quite a few times.

'Why did I not hear what the postman said?' he said.

That really threw me because I had clearly heard the words the postman had uttered, and Harris had been standing next to me.

\*\*\*

We reached our destination and I turned the car so that it faced the lodge. Harris quickly opened the door and leaped out; I followed as he ran around to the side of the lodge. He stopped at the reek of turf, the symmetry of which I had admired yesterday, and to my utter astonishment began clawing at the sods and tossing them to one side.

'Give me a hand. We must remove the turf from the reek.'

We set to the task with determination and, to my amazement, after twenty or more sods had been removed, I saw the top of a yellow sack sticking from the pile. More and more sacks followed, as we worked our way through the reek, and soon we had fifteen yellow and ten green sacks lying on the ground. At a rough calculation there was at least £100,000 lying there in front of us.

'How many Morris Minors would that get you, Jonathan?'

He was at it again, reading my thoughts.

'So Nugent did steal the money?'

'Yes, and in the process I have learned a valuable lesson – always trust your instincts, despite what the pronouncements of others might be. I allowed my superior intellect to be deflected by accepting the general consensus of lesser minds.'

Superior intellect! Lesser minds! What could I say?

'From the first moment, I was certain it was Nugent but allowed my considerations to be compromised by flawed arguments. Take the evidence of the postman.'

'What about the postman? I was standing next to you when he told us he had seen Nugent at the lodge every morning for the last week. Nor only that, but he saw him walk past his house on the Friday or Saturday before the robbery.'

'But that is where you are wrong. He said he had seen the car parked at the lakeside every morning as he cycled by. He never said he saw Nugent.'

'Did he not see him walk past his house as he was coming out the gate?'

'Indeed he did, but Nugent was walking in the wrong direction. Why was Nugent walking away from the village?'

'Going for a stroll?' I suggested.

'I'm certain we will find that one of Nugent's fishing buddies lives further out that road. He had arranged some time back to borrow his car for a few days. He would have given him some plausible excuse about his own car being broken down. This was the part of the investigation that caused me most difficulty; I could not figure out how Nugent managed to get back to Oughterard from Finlough on the Friday he commenced his so-called fishing holiday while his sports car was still parked outside the lodge. How did he do it? The chance remark by the postman, of seeing him walk out of the village, led me to believe he was going to meet someone. I am certain the local Guards, on making enquiries, will find the person who loaned

Nugent the car.'

'When did you realise the sacks were hidden in the turf reek?'

'They had to be in a secure place close by, hidden from prying eyes. When you talked about the starlings and putting more turf on the fire at the cottage this afternoon, it suddenly struck me.'

'What struck you?'

'Come, and I will show you.'

'When we were walking past the front door of the fishing lodge yesterday, do you remember looking through the window and seeing the turf stacked up each side of the fireplace and more turf lying against a wall on the far side of the room?'

'Yes.'

'Did you notice the old bird's nest lying in the fireplace?'

'I can't recall, but what does that have to do with the matter at hand?'

'It proves that a fire has not been lit in the lodge for months. How could Nugent, or anyone else, sleep in a cold stone hut in the freezing cold without lighting a fire? Why did he have piles of turf lined up near the fireplace and along some of the walls and never use them? You remarked, Jonathan, at the symmetry of the turf reek and how well it looked. But if the reek was still intact, where did all the turf inside the lodge come from?

'There could only be one explanation. Nugent had removed the turf sods from the reek some weeks earlier in anticipation of the forthcoming robbery. It was a simple thing for him to return here, with the stolen sacks, and place them in the space he had created within the reek. Once the sacks were placed there, he rebuilt the reek to make it appear as if it had never been disturbed. He brought the sods of turf that were left over into the lodge and placed them against the wall or near the fireplace.'

\*\*\*

We put the sacks into the car and drove back to Mannane. I slowed down almost to a crawl as we passed the Major's house. I need not have bothered, as there was no sign of him. The house was in darkness and he was either in bed or had gone out.

'We must telephone Hennessy straight away and tell him what has happened,' said Harris, with urgency in his voice.

'It will mean using the phone at the Emporium,' I said.

'Will you try and distract Miss Mannion after she connects my call and prevent her listening in?' he asked.

We entered the Emporium and Harris went over to Miss Mannion and politely asked if he could use the telephone. He gave her the number and she retreated to the tiny back room to make the connection. She came out and said, 'Your call is now connected, pick up the phone at the end of the counter and speak into it.'

She was about to retreat to the tiny room again when I called her name. Harris nodded at me in a knowing way.

'Yes, Jonathan, what can I do for you?'

I, stupidly, had not considered what I would say. She stood facing me, smiling; her eyes staring into mine. In desperation, I blurted out the first thing that came into my head.

'The Major gave me a loan of his car for a few days but I have to give it back to him on Wednesday.'

'And you want to take me for a drive some evening? I would like that very much.'

In desperation, I nodded my head up and down and then sideways. I was lost for words at this turn of events.

'Why don't you and I go for a drive into Galway tomorrow afternoon? I can get Mary Byrne to run the shop for the few hours we will be away.'

I smiled at her, speechless. It had always been my intention to ask her out one day but now she had taken the first step and I was somewhat put out by it. She had trapped me; what could I do? To add to my woes, she took my silence as an affirmation of her suggestion.

'That's settled then. Pick me up tomorrow at three o'clock.'

I was cornered and, being too much of a gentleman, was reluctant to say no. Harris, meanwhile, had finished the phone call and said to me as we walked to the door, 'The Inspector will be calling to the cottage later this evening. '

We were just about to exit the door when the melodious voice of Helen Mannion rang out: 'Three o' clock tomorrow, Jonathan, don't be late.'

'What's all that about?' asked Harris.

'I don't want to talk about it,' I replied.

# CHAPTER 7

Monday evening was drawing to a close and through the front room window I watched a farmer walking in a nearby field, counting his sheep and cattle. The Inspector arrived soon afterwards and, without invitation, sat down in his usual seat; our habitual tenant. He expressed his gratitude to Harris but marred it somewhat by saying, 'You know I was coming to the conclusion that Nugent was my man but was holding off while investigations were still in progress. Your phone call more or less confirmed my suspicions. I knew the money had to be hidden nearby and it would have been just a matter of time before I found it.'

I just could not let this go and spoke up, not that Harris needed me to.

'Yes, I'm sure you would have got there eventually, but where is Nugent?'

'We arrested him at Sweeney's Hotel in Oughterard where he had gone to stay while his house was being examined by the forensic people. His reaction was incredible; total and absolute denial. You should have seen the look of bewilderment on his face when I and two uniformed Guards confronted him. I do believe he thought he had gotten away with it. He denied everything and insisted he had been at the lodge all the time.

'You were correct in your assumption that he had borrowed a friend's car for the week. That has now been confirmed. He must have parked his sports car in front of the fishing lodge on the Friday afternoon and walked into Leenane to his friend's house to collect that car. It is a seven-mile walk from the fishing lodge to Leenane and it must have taken a couple of hours to cover that distance. He was taking a bit of a risk as he could have been spotted by someone,' said the Inspector.

'A slight risk and a long walk well worth taking considering the prize on offer,' replied Harris, 'but it mattered little if he was observed walking that road to Leenane. You can be certain he was carrying a fishing rod and, to a casual passer-by, he was an angler making his way further up the valley to fish.'

'You are right. I never thought of that. Much later that evening, when it was dark, he drove back to his house in Oughterard using the borrowed car. He parked it in his enclosed back garden, went into his house and remained there for the week.'

'So, did he admit to everything?' asked Harris

'When I revealed that the cash had been discovered in the turf reek, he was stunned and could scarcely believe what I was saying. He muttered something like, "Who could have hidden the money there? It certainly wasn't me." He continued to deny everything until I informed him that the fingerprints found on the sacks at the lodge matched those on his sports car and were most definitely his.'

'These would be the sacks that you have not yet seen and that are still in the boot of the car which is parked outside the door?'

'Yes,' replied Hennessy, without blinking an eye, 'the very ones.'

'You continue to amaze me, Inspector. You are becoming artful in the game of deception. Fingerprints indeed.'

'In the fight against crime, the Queensbury Rules don't always apply,' said the Inspector, with an impish grin on his face. 'He made a full statement, confessing to everything.'

'How did he know the sacks of money were being transferred to the bank at Oughterard?' I asked.

'He lives next door to the bank and, over the years, had become friendly with the bank manager,' the Inspector explained. 'They even go fishing together. A few weeks ago, while having a drink in a local pub, the manager inadvertently let slip some details about the upcoming movement of bank notes to Oughterard from the other banks. He must have said they were being delivered to be sent for incineration.

'Once Nugent heard this, he began to make plans. He was friendly with the local Guards and was able to find out a bit more information from one of them. This Guard told him that all leave had been cancelled for Thursday and Friday in two weeks' time and that extra Guards were being transferred into Oughterard for those days. He had no idea why, but Nugent knew the reason.

'The prospect of such an event happening next door to his house and the possibility of getting his hands on so much untraceable money was just too much for him. He is not in financial difficulties but saw a life-changing opportunity to amass a colossal amount of money.'

'There is one thing I still don't understand,' I said.

'Only one thing, Jonathan?' said Harris, smiling.

'Yes. You mentioned, Inspector, that there were three different brands of cigarettes in the ashtray, which indicate three people had been on the premises. Surely his accomplices, whoever they may be, should also be arrested.'

'Yes, all in good time, but it is of little consequence at the moment now that the case has been solved. Once we have cross-examined Nugent, we will get the names of his accomplices.'

Harris turned to the Inspector and said, 'But there were no accomplices.'

'What are you saying? Of course there are accomplices.'

'I must beg to differ,' replied Harris. 'That first morning after we arrived at Nugent's office, I examined the ashtray and it contained, as you say, three different brands of cigarette butts. On closer inspection, I could see that they were at least two weeks old and some had brown discolouring that hinted at beer having been spilled on them at some point in time.

'I am certain, that, some days earlier, when drinking in some pub, Nugent emptied the contents of a full ashtray into a bag and then brought it back to his house. When he got home, he emptied the contents into the ashtray he had in his house. My study of cigarettes and ash has been most useful to me at certain times. In the case of the Bohemian Stockbroker, the light texture of the cigarette ash was his undoing. I have written on booklet on the subject.'

I smiled to myself. Was there anything he had not written about?

'How did you conclude the money was hidden in the reek?' asked Hennessy.

'You may thank Jonathan for that. He was going outside to get turf for the fire and in passing mentioned that the starlings were building their nests. It was then I realised that the reek outside the lodge had never been touched but yet there were stacks of turf in that front room. The old bird's nest lying in the fireplace meant a fire had not been lit there for some time. It just didn't make any sense. Would Nugent spend a week in a cold, rundown lodge without lighting a fire? I don't believe he would.'

But there was something that still perplexed me and I asked, 'What was it you saw when you went out to the small garden to examine the kitchen window that made you wonder, as you said.'

'Nugent had to stage a break-in to make the robbery look like an outside job, but he made the cardinal error of breaking the glass in the wrong place. From just a cursory look, it was obvious to me that anyone putting their arm in to reach up to the window clasp would be unable to do so. It would be impossible for any arm to reach that far.

'It may seem incredible, but in many of the cases I have dealt with during my career, it is the simple mistakes that let criminals down. The small moment it took to stage the break-in through the kitchen window was just as important as all the laborious hours spent breaking through the wall. Attention to detail is the hallmark of the exceptional criminal.'

'And you immediately noticed the mistake he had made when breaking the window?'

'Of course.'

\*\*\*

The weeks passed by and the longer stretch in the days came in quietly and gently. We would soon be able to go for long walks in the evenings. For some time, it had been on my mind to get way for a few days. A visit to a hotel near the sea would be admirable. I arranged for Harris and myself to head down to the southeast of the country. What better place to lie low for a few days. How was I to know that the Man in the White Suit would be there?

# The Man in The White Suit

## CHAPTER 1

In the early mornings, I sat outside, weather permitting, at the rear of the hotel, on the sheltered side, and had my breakfast served to me. My gaze took in the landscaped gardens, that were such a feature of the wonderful hotel and I savoured the peace and tranquility. If I turned my head to the left, momentarily forsaking the magnificent garden views, I was rewarded by the sight of a most wonderful golden beach, stretching away in the distance towards the town of Wexford. There was a well-trodden pathway that wandered from the garden and made its way through a steep sand dune before leading down onto the beach.

To my right, the small port of Rosslare was just visible and I took great delight in watching the comings and goings of the fishing boats. The previous day, a ship steamed into the harbour; a delightful and unexpected sight. My table had to be the greatest observation place in the whole world as I could see all the comings and goings from it.

He was here again on this morning, the man in the white suit, taking his constitutional, but this time coming from the opposite direction of yesterday. He moved at a leisurely pace towards me, walking near the sea, avoiding the fine soft sand. As he strolled along, he raised his left hand to the brim of his straw boater hat to protect it from the slight breeze blowing in from the sea. Just as he drew level with me, he glanced over and raised his silver-top walking cane in acknowledgment. I raised my hand and smiled as he passed along.

\*\*\*

'Good morning, Jonathan, I knew I would find you here in your usual place. We are all such creatures of habit.'

It was Harris. He had already been out and about, and I observed three daily newspapers tucked under his left arm. A man intent on serious reading, I surmised. From the dining room, a waitress emerged to take his order.

'Just a pot of strong coffee and some toast,' he said.

She raised an eyebrow in surprise. The breakfast here was renowned and few if any passed on it. Harris was an exception. He sat down opposite me and, taking the papers in turn, quickly read the headlines on the front page of each of them.

'That scoundrel, Nelson, is still at large and dominating the front pages. Why is it they are unable to find him?'

I nodded at the news that the notorious Nelson, who had escaped from the Four Courts in Dublin while at a court hearing, was still at large. Who would have imagined that, in the month of May 1954, in this idyllic country where so little of note occurred, a dangerous gangster wanted for at least three murders and numerous bank robberies would still be on the run and evading all attempts at recapture.

Although the escape had taken place six days earlier, it still commanded the headlines. Even in the quiet village of Mannane, in County Galway, where Harris and I were residing at the cottage, he was the topic of conversation before we'd left for our short break in County Wexford.

'Big jewel theft at Roundwood House out near Wexford yesterday evening.'

He read the article quickly, to himself, and then absentmindedly looked out towards the sea, evaluating the written words. I knew his methods and the secret signs that played on his face when that great brain of his was analysing a problem.

'Inside job, of course.'

I smiled to myself at Harris' throwaway remark, but I knew it was a serious observation and more than likely true. He had a way of assimilating information, running it through that weird brain of his, and coming up with solutions that astonished people. When he was in Balfour Street, our good friend, Inspector Andrew Fleming of Scotland Yard, often called to consult him on difficult cases.

He had now moved onto the classified and personal section of the *Irish Independent*. There was much smiling and then a whoop of delight. He had found what he has been looking for – a little gem in the adverts.

'Jonathan, listen to this. *Would the young lady who mistakenly took my suitcase and overcoat from the 5.30 p.m. train from Dublin to Sligo please contact me.* He even leaves a phone number.'

More laughter; I knew I was in for another ten minutes of this at least. It was remarkable to me how such frivolous items intrigued this man who was the most famous private investigator in all of Britain and Ireland. Even in the Cambridge days, between the wars, he took enormous delight in reading the classifieds in *The Times*.

'Good morning, gentlemen. Are they looking after you?' It was John, the manager of the family-owned hotel.

'Everything is just wonderful,' replied Harris. 'This is a splendid place.'

'Your first visit?'

'Yes,' I answered, 'but there will be many more.'

He smiled and nodded his head in approval at the complimentary remarks and said, 'Will you be heading over to Ashford Manor to view the painting and sculpture exhibition?'

This was a reference to the Christie's of London auction of Irish works of art which was set to take place two days later and which had previews for today and tomorrow. It was a major event that attracted not only people from Ireland, but from the Continent and Great Britain as well.

'I imagine we will call in and have a look around,' said Harris.

'Is it far from here?' I asked. 'Could we walk to it?'

'You could walk there in less than half an hour. Call at the reception desk on your way out; I will leave a few catalogues there for you.'

The fact that we were within walking distance of Ashford Manor was good news to me as I was loath to move the Morris Minor from the hotel car park where it had remained since our arrival. The expenditure of £475 on this car had been one of my better investments. Even Harris agreed.

***

It was just short of eleven o'clock as we strolled up the long, winding avenue that led to the entrance door of Ashford Manor. The large sign placed strategically on the front lawn read, *Admission by catalogue only, price 2/6*. This was most certainly a deterrent to the average holiday maker.

'Be on your best behavior, Jonathan, we shall be rubbing shoulders with the aristocracy. No hoi polloi here,' Harris said, laughing.

The splendid and imposing three-storey Victorian house was set in a secluded estate of woods and farmland. It was a magnificent place; a monument to a long past golden age. Outside the main entrance door, and a little to the right, so that access to the building was not impeded, a small black lorry was parked. Three men were engaged in extracting what was obviously one of the items in the sale – a life-size statue of the famous American president, George Washington, standing upright, his left arm raised skywards. They carefully carried the statue into the house under the supervision and direction of the man in the white suit.

'How interesting,' said Harris, 'never for one moment did I think he would be selling something at the auction. How odd.'

He said no more, but I could tell he was somewhat perplexed.

***

On entering the main door we are directed, by a judiciously positioned sign, to a room to the right where the works of famous Irish sculptors were displayed. For as long as I could remember, I had been an admirer of this form of art, which connected with my fascination with Egyptian tombs and the burial grounds of the Pharaohs. I had spent four years in the Valley of the Kings prior to my arrival in Ireland the previous September. A glance at the catalogue convinced me that I would not be disappointed with the exhibition.

Harris, I was certain, would find little to interest him here, but I admired his unstinting generosity in accompanying me. The magnificent large room, with six tall and majestic windows, had been enriched by the wonderful sculptures on display. They varied in size from figurines to full-size works. We spent some time looking at the exhibits as we moved slowly along.

After a while, we noticed that, at the far end of the room, there was one other person who was fully engrossed in measuring one of the sculpted figures. At first I assumed it was one of the exhibition staff, making last-minute adjustments, but there was something odd about this man's behavior, something out of place. Armed with a measuring tape, he was diligently calculating the dimensions of a statue and jotting the results down in a notebook. Most peculiar, I thought. This certainly was a man on a mission who had more than a passing interest in the life-size figure of the Greek god whose name escaped me.

So engrossed was he in his work that he did not discern our presence. Then, sensing us, he turned his head and immediately sprang backwards in surprise, just as a child might do when caught stealing biscuits from a tin. I was certain he was up to no good. There was guilt written all over his face, or maybe it was embarrassment. He smiled, wistfully, as he passed by and doffed his straw boater hat. It was the man in the white suit.

To my surprise, Harris had taken a keen interest in a figurine of a Roman soldier and was examining it in a critical way. 'It would look well on the mantelpiece in the front room,' he said.

'Yes, it would,' I replied, not sure if he was intent on buying it.

'We'll come along to the auction the day after tomorrow and see if there is much interest in it.'

I had already looked it up in the catalogue and saw that the Roman soldier was an expensive young man – £100 to be exact. That would pay for four weeks' holidays in Kelly's Hotel! I also noted that the auction was due to commence at 11 a.m. and that the first items to go under the hammer would be the sculptures.

'I notice from the catalogue that the figurine you are interested in is number four in the auction list. 'In that case, we will make sure we are here before eleven o'clock on the day,' said Harris.

# CHAPTER 2

It was evening time and we were sitting in comfortable armchairs adjacent to the dining room, from where we had just exited following a most delightful meal. In all my travels, I would be hard pressed to recall when I had last eaten food of such quality. It was that in-between time when one has partaken of a splendid meal and is contemplating a short stroll before bedtime, to help allay that full feeling when one has overindulged. Then, later, a final nightcap and the pleasant anticipation of a charming bed with crisp, white, linen sheets. Such bliss.

Harris had his pipe firmly clenched between his teeth and was contemplating the large glass of Jameson whiskey that lay on the table in front of us when he whispered, 'Jonathan, did you notice that our mysterious friend, in the white suit, who was acting somewhat suspiciously at the Christie's preview this morning has just walked out the front door?'

'Yes, I saw him pass along.'

'Is it not strange that someone who is a resident at the hotel would seem to spend much of his time on the beach, or walking the roads near the golf course. Odd behaviour, do you not think, for someone who has the use of the hotel's many facilities and yet is rarely here except at mealtimes? What do you make of him, Jonathan? A strange fellow, you must admit.'

Swirling the whiskey gently around the glass, I mulled over this statement. 'Yes, indeed, a strange fellow, but one of substance, I would venture to say.'

'Really? You do surprise me, Jonathan.'

'Undoubtedly here for the auction and assuredly intent on bidding for that statue he was examining this morning.'

'I agree with your conclusion, but a man of substance? Surely not.'

'You must have noticed the old Etonian tie? Obviously an educated fellow from a sound family.'

'Splendid, Jonathan, well spotted. There is hope for you yet. Anything else catch your eye?'

'The white suit,' I continued, 'is distinctive and of a kind preferred by artists and those who engage in such activities. At first, I had formed an opinion that he, perhaps, was a representative of the house of Christie's, over from London.'

'How discerning you are, Jonathan, please do continue.'

'Well, having considered everything and his extraordinary behavior at Ashford Manor this morning, I have concluded that he is a dealer in fine arts and has a distinct interest, as I already said, in making a bid for the Greek god he was examining. He has to be a man of means to be capable of mingling with the affluent clientele who turn up at Christie's auctions. Old school, I'm certain, ex Etonian, as his tie indicates. Possibly has a fine art premises in Mayfair. These sort usually do.'

Harris was staring at me in a peculiar manner; it was most disconcerting.

'Dear me, Jonathan, you could not be further off the mark. The man is a cheat, an imposter, a philistine.'

'Steady on, Harris, how can you even contemplate such thoughts? You have not even spoken to him.'

Neither had I, for that matter.

'You must have noticed him in the dining room, partaking of his soup? Surely you observed how he tilted his bowl towards himself to scoop out the last few spoonful's? No Etonian worth his salt would be so remiss in etiquette. That white suit he constantly wears is dated or, should I say, outdated. Such attire does not become a person endeavouring to pass themselves off as one of means. His shirt collar is frayed, and his brown shoes are badly worn, and have already been repaired on two occasions.

'His fingernails are not those of a gentleman. They have never been manicured and are broken and chipped. He is not the professional person he endeavours to make himself out to be, but earns his living, I would guess, by some sort of manual exertion.'

Harris, obviously noticing the look of dismay on my face, said, 'But you are correct in your acute observation regarding the tie with the black and turquoise strips. It is indeed that of Eton. Did you, by chance, notice the tie pin attached to it.'

I perked up at this for I had observed it. 'Yes, I did. It had the figure of a black lion.'

'Precisely, the famous figure of the black lion of Harrow College. Which begs the question – did this gentleman attend both colleges? I very much doubt it. He is an uncouth philistine who purchased the tie and pin as a job lot somewhere. I would say at a house clearing sale.

'There is something sinister afoot here. I feel there may be bad business going down, Jonathan. Perhaps he is a common thief, here to steal some of the hotel's splendid paintings, or maybe he intends ransacking the rooms and making off with the fine jewelry worn by some of the ladies in the dining room this evening. He may even be intent on stealing the statue he was measuring this morning.'

'But why would he measure a statue?' I asked.

'Indeed, an interesting question.'

'Is it not odd that he is trying to sell the George Washington statue while at the same time is interested in the Greek god?'

'I agree that does seem peculiar. I noticed him in the hotel car park this evening, before dinner,' continued Harris, 'standing next to the small black van. It has a British registration number. Maybe I am misjudging him and it is his intention to purchase that statue of the Greek god and transport it back to England. But there is something not right about all this, and yet I can't put my finger on it. A visit to the auction might just be interesting.'

I nodded in agreement even though it would mean forsaking my morning walk on the beach. I am a dedicated creature of habit who, at times, had to give way to the whims of Harris. However, there would be the compensation of a roadside walk to Ashford Manor. Not quite the same as a walk on the delightful beach, however.

# CHAPTER 3

At the top of the main street, tucked away at the corner, no more than five hundred yards from the hotel, was a family-run grocery store and newsagents. It was a useful place to purchase the small items that were so important to everyday survival, such as boxes of matches, bullseye sweets and newspapers. Numerous assorted books of varying size and age, and magazines covering many topics were laid out on the wooden counter.

I was there, just before lunchtime, at the behest of Harris who had found himself in the precarious position of being in immediate danger of running short of matches. Such a happening would be a calamity. To my surprise, our much discussed and somewhat maligned hotel resident, the man in the white suit, was also in the shop. Nothing unusual in that, but I could not help but overhear the conversation he was having with a young shop assistant.

He was standing at the long counter calling out the items he required from a shopping list. I raised an eyebrow at the nature of the goods requested and, while surreptitiously browsing the magazines, unashamedly eavesdropped. Bread, butter, jam, cheese, milk, bacon, and eggs; the list went on. I was staggered at the sheer length of it. I noticed his accent was that of one from the East End of London. What in heaven's name was going on, I wondered. This fellow, like myself, was partaking of three magnificent meals a day, and yet felt disposed to purchase such day-to-day grocery items. It made no sense. In fact, within the hour, he would be tucking into a fine lunch at the hotel.

Another assistant handed me the six boxes of matches requested and I left the scene, pondering on what I had just witnessed, and started back for the hotel.

*\*\*\**

I found Harris relaxing in a large armchair, adjacent to the reception area, polluting the air with clouds of tobacco smoke. I related the details of my recent encounter in the shop and the peculiar purchases of our fellow hotel resident to him. To my astonishment, he leaped up from the armchair.

'When did this happen?' he asked.

'Less than ten minutes ago. I've just left him in the shop. '

'So, he should be making his way back to the hotel?'

'Yes, I imagine so.'

'And he did not pass you on the road on your way back?'

'No, but he may have cut across from the shop and walked back along the beach. There is an entrance there.'

'Come, Jonathan, let's see if he's outside on the roadway.'

Harris, all action, rushed to the main door. Following closely behind, I was almost bowled over when he abruptly turned around and retreated.

'Stay, Jonathan. Don't move. He's just walked past the hotel and is heading in the direction of the golf course.'

*\*\*\**

We waited for a moment or so and then exited through the door in pursuit. He was an easy quarry to trail. Unsuspecting, he walked at a leisurely pace, carrying two large brown shopping bags crammed full of his recent purchases. We lingered behind, nonchalantly looking over the fields towards the sea. He was in no hurry and, yet, there was a purpose in his demeanour that indicated he was expecting to rendezvous with someone in the locality.

This was the road we took each evening for our after-dinner walk. It went past the golf course and turned back, further on, at a headland. Just before the golf course there was a caravan field which I knew was closed for the season. The notice on the padlock gate indicating it would be reopening in June had caught my eye on one of the evening walks.

He crossed the road and we stopped and leaned against the stone wall and again we looked over the fields to the sea. We glanced towards him and observed that he was gingerly putting the bags of groceries through the lower section of the four-bar wooden gate that served as an entrance to the caravan field. Once he had passed the bags through and placed them on the ground, he climbed over the gate and leaped to the other side. He picked up the two grocery bags and made his way across the field.

There were a few caravans standing at the further end of the field, near the sand dunes. I assumed they belonged to the owner and were available for rent all year round. In the summertime, I imagined, when the field reopened, it would be thronged with touring caravans.

Harris and I watched as the man in the white suit steadily made his way towards a green and yellow caravan that was parked at the furthest end, close to the sand dunes. Next to the caravan was the small, black, open-backed van. We had moved from our position at the stone wall, crossed the road, and were standing at the side of the wooden gate. We watched as he approached the caravan and lay the grocery bags down on the steps that led to the door. Then he went to the curtained window on the left-hand side of the door and rapped on it with his knuckles.

The curtain moved a little and just as quickly settled back in place. The door of the caravan was opened, and a hand appeared and beckoned the visitor to enter. Picking up the grocery bags, the man in the white suit entered through the door which was immediately closed behind him.

'Did you see anything when the door opened?' asked Harris.

'I just saw a beckoning hand.'

'This is most peculiar,' said Harris. 'Who is the man in the caravan?'

'How do you know it is a man? It may be a woman,' I said, pointedly.

'Surely you noticed the size of the hand? It is most definitely that of a very tall man.'

This was just too much for me and I asked, 'How can you judge the height of a person and conclude it is a man from just looking at a hand?'

'It is a proven fact that the span of a person's hand is one tenth of their height. The Vitruvian drawing by Leonardo the Vinci, some five hundred years ago, illustrated that conclusion. His theory has been authenticated by modern-day science. I only got a glimpse of the hand for a few seconds, but I would confidently estimate the span to be to be seven or eight inches in length. That indicates a person of seventy to eighty inches in height; unlikely to be a woman. I'm certain probability testing would indicate it is a man.'

'How do you know all this stuff?'

'You should take an interest in the *Encyclopedia Britannica*. It's full of that 'stuff', as you so nicely put it.'

That told me off.

\*\*\*

There was nothing more to be achieved by loitering near the field, so we walked further along the road and came to a small entrance to the beach. Everything in this small village led to the beach. There was little conversation as we made our way back to the hotel. In the distance we watched three fishing boats navigate their way into Rosslare Harbour. They would be out fishing again the next day.

Back at the hotel, we sat in the garden. Harris was unusually quiet; no doubt going over in his mind the scene we had just witnessed at the caravan field. I sat in my comfortable chair in the beautiful garden, reflecting on how we had come to this hotel for a short break and walked straight into another peculiar happening. Were we the only guests to have noticed this strange man in white? It would seem so. On the other hand, Harris, with his discerning and brilliant mind, always noticed things that others failed to see.

After a late lunch, we sat in the foyer re-reading the newspapers. I must have dozed off for I was awakened by a hand shaking my shoulder.

'Just thought you would like to know that our mutual friend has driven into the hotel car park in the black open-backed van. He obviously has a key for that padlock at the caravan field. I wonder why he moved the van? What do you think, Jonathan?' Harris asked.

'It is quite simple,' I replied. 'There can be but one explanation. He came over from England, for the auction, with the intention of buying that statue he was examining yesterday and selling the one he brought with him. He has parked the van nearby in readiness for tomorrow's auction. If he is successful in his bid, he will have Christie's crate the statue for him, place it in the van, and transport it back to England. I think we have been tilting at windmills. '

'You are quite right, Jonathan. It might be as simple as that. But, then, experience has taught me that things are never as simple as they seem.'

# CHAPTER 4

The weather forecast was accurate and I woke early in the morning to the sound of rain beating against the windows. It was auction day and looked like it would be a damp walk to Ashford Manor. Having breakfasted in the dining room on my own – no sitting outside today – I wandered about the hotel looking for Harris. I eventually located him in the conservatory, reading the newspapers and drinking black coffee.

'I think we should be on our way to the auction. It begins in forty minutes. Will I take the car?'

'No, let us walk. A bit of rain never did anyone any harm.'

We set off at a brisk pace, our heads protected by the two large umbrellas we had obtained at the reception desk.

***

We were ten minutes early and I made my way determinedly towards the front row of chairs.

'Jonathan! Jonathan!' called Harris. 'Let's sit back here.'

I came back, not happy with this turn of events. 'Why sit here when there are far better seats at the front?'

'It is always imperative to be able to see your enemies.'

'Enemies?'

'Well, not enemies, but those people who might be bidding for my Roman figurine. Good to have them to the front. That way I can watch their every action.'

I realised he was right, but there was no way I was going to tell him that.

'You are quite right, Jonathan, it does make sense.'

I shook my head in amazement. He was at it again; reading my thoughts. How did he do this, I wondered.

The Roman figurine was number four on the list and Harris was very pleased to have it knocked down to £75 for him.

Then I felt Harris grip my arm tightly. 'Look who has just come in.'

I looked over to where he indicated and saw the man in the white suit take a seat a few rows in front of us, on the left-hand side.

The auction progressed at pace, and then the George Washington statue was announced as the next lot for sale. There was some interest in the statue and bidding was brisk. Within minutes, and after eight bids, there were two interested parties remaining in the contest. One was a very well-dressed, middle-aged lady and the other, to our astonishment, was the man in the white suit.

'What's going on, Harris? He is bidding for his own statue, the one he put into the auction to be sold. Are you allowed to do that?'

'You are assuming the statue is owned by him.'

'But did we not see it being man-handled from the back of the small lorry that was parked near the front door on our arrival for the auction preview? That was surely his lorry?'

'Yes, it was his lorry, and I do believe the statue belongs to him. You can be certain the paperwork presented to the Christie's representatives is in order and the provenance is genuine. However, our mutual friend is only following the instructions given to him by some other party.'

The bidding for the statue slowed somewhat and it was finally knocked down for £300. It was sold to the man in the white suit. I sat there, bemused by what I had just witnessed.

'You are quite right, Jonathan, you could buy a good second-hand Morris Minors for that and still have change.'

He was at it again, reading my mind.

I was standing up, just about to leave the room, when Harris said, 'Hold on a moment, Jonathan, the next lot to be sold is the statue of the Greek god, the one our friend was measuring the other day. It will be interesting to see what happens next.'

The bidding began and the man in the white suit immediately got up and walked out of the room.

*\*\**

You had to admire the efficiency of the backroom people at the auction. When Harris went to pay for the figurine, not only was it ready for him, it was encased in a small, wooden box, wrapped neatly in brown paper and covered in tape bearing the name *Christie's of London*. There was a certain style about the wrapping that was distinctive and to be admired.

'Are you taking your purchase abroad?' asked the official.

'No. Why do you ask?'

'If it were going abroad, I would attach clearance documents to it and other paperwork that would alleviate the necessity of going through Customs and Excise.

*\*\**

It rained heavily for the remainder of the day, so we sat indoors, reading and looking out the windows at the cars and people that were out and about. I picked up one of the newspapers Harris had discarded and, settling into the armchair, began reading. There was talk of a general election and this had relegated the hunt for the notorious master criminal, Nelson, to the inside pages.

It is quite remarkable that when a description of a wanted person is published in the newspapers, how many sightings are reported from all over the place. He had been sighted in Donegal, right down to the other end of the country in County Kerry. My opinion was that he was sunning himself on a beach in the south of Spain; when one has the money, ill-gotten or otherwise, anything is possible.

Harris was smoking his pipe and staring, absentmindedly, out the window, when, to my amazement, he said, 'Jonathan, you are an intelligent and perceptive person.'

I was taken aback by the unexpected words and wallowed unashamedly at this compliment for a moment or so.

'Now, can you figure this out for me – a man wearing a white suit that is the worse for wear tries to pass himself off as an old Etonian. He goes to an auction and spends £300 – a vast amount of money – on a hideous statue that, in fact, belongs to him or one of his acquaintances. Yet, when it comes up for auction, he completely ignores the statue of the Greek god that he had been measuring a few days back. We follow him to a caravan field that has been closed for a few months and observe him deliver groceries to someone in a caravan at the end of the field. Can you make any sense of that?'

I couldn't, and did not even try, allowing the questions to slip by as if they were rhetorical. Yet, it was very strange. Who was the tall man in the caravan, afraid to show his face?

Then I thought of something and said, 'Perhaps our Etonian friend and the man in the caravan intend stealing the cash takings at the auction. Quite a few people will settle their accounts in cash.'

'It's possible, but it does not explain why someone is hiding in a caravan. No, something else, more sinister, is about to happen.'

\*\*\*

It was midafternoon and had finally stopped raining. We decided to take advantage of this change in the weather and go for a walk.

'I would be interested in having another look at the caravan field,' said Harris.

It was as we had left it the previous evening, or so it seemed at first glance. The black van was not there. The curtains in the caravan, that had been closed the previous day, were now pulled back. We climbed the padlocked gate and walked in the direction of the caravan. Harris boldly made his way to the caravan door and knocked loudly on it. There was no response. We looked through the window and could see that it was empty. Whoever had been in there was gone.

'We are too late. Now we will never know who was here,' he said.

Harris moved around to the back of the caravan, looking intently at the ground. I followed closely behind. Lying at the back of the caravan, hidden from the view of those passing along the road, was a large smashed timber crate.

'This is very odd,' I said. 'Surely this is the crate that the statue of George Washington was stored in following its purchase at the auction.'

'It certainly looks like it.'

'But why has it been removed from the crate?' I asked.

'Look, Jonathan, over here. Do you see that the ground has recently been disturbed? Something has been dragged along here over to that big sand dune.'

I looked at where he was pointing and could clearly see the marks on the damp ground. There was a trail leading from the side of the caravan to the dunes. My immediate thought was that foul play had taken place. Were these the marks of a body being pulled along the sandy ground? It certainly looked like it. I was letting my imagination run wild. Steady on, I thought.

We followed the tracks which stopped abruptly at the bottom of the nearest sand dune. The sand was very fine and soft and I could see it had recently been disturbed. Someone had been digging here. Harris went down on his knees and began scooping out the fine sand with his bare hands. It was not a difficult task as the sand had only recently been filled in at this spot. I watched, transfixed, unable to move. Digging for tombs and ruins while I was in Egypt was simple compared to what was going on here. At any moment, I expected the outline of a body to appear.

'Help me, Jonathan, I think I have found something,' Harris said.

There was nothing for it but to get on my hands and knees next to him. Working away with my bare hands, I began throwing sand in all directions. Suddenly, there was a loud gasp from Harris and I looked across to where he was digging. I drew back in horror when I saw a hand sticking out from the sand. It is strange how you react in these situations. The first thing that entered my head was that the hand appeared to be seven or eight inches long. Weird! Was I getting like Harris?

# CHAPTER 5

'My heavens!' I said, in a shocked voice. 'Someone has been murdered and buried here.'

'Steady on, Jonathan, take a closer look.'

I looked over and immediately saw that what had been uncovered was not a human hand. It was the hand of a statue, and just had to be the one the man in the white suit had acquired at the auction some hours earlier. After a bit more digging, the entire statue of George Washington was revealed. I stood there, mystified, wondering what it all meant.

'There is nothing more we can do here,' said Harris. 'We may as well go back to the hotel.'

\*\*\*

The May sun was in decline. Weather-wise it had been a mixed day and it was our last day at Kelly's. We would be returning to the cottage in Mannane the following day. There was still sufficient warmth from the sun for us to loll on deckchairs that, notwithstanding our weight – which had been immensely added to over the previous few days – endured the extreme pressure on their colourful canvas.

My mind, like that of Harris, was still occupied by our very recent experience at the caravan field. For the life of me, I could still make nothing of it. Why pay £300 for a statue and then bury it?

'You know, the commission charge for the transaction will be at least £45. Why put an object into an auction and buy it back yourself and give £45 to Christie's for the pleasure of doing business with them?'

'I know, Jonathan, it makes no sense, and yet there has to be a good reason for it.'

Harris was not at ease in the deckchair and it came as no surprise when he said, 'I've had enough of this, Jonathan, I am going for a walk on the beach. Would you care to join me?'

Our usual stroll would normally take us to the left as we exited the garden for the beach but, this time, for a change, we headed right, in the direction of Rosslare village. Harris was very quiet, obviously still brooding over the strange episode at the caravan field. Every now and then, as we strolled along, I could hear him whisper, 'But why bury it?'

Such was his unquestioning ability and mathematical genius, he could never comprehend why problems could not be solved instantly. He could be very hard on himself, especially when things were not going his way. It concerned me, as I knew only too well where this could lead to. He had a propensity to be depressed when his methods did not bring results.

In the distance, I could see the fishing boats heading back to Rosslare Harbour. Away from them, but still visible on the horizon, a big ship was steaming along, heading for England, or some land further away.

'Must be interesting to work on a ship, going back and forth across the sea and calling into different ports,' I remarked.

'Who is going back and forth across the sea?' Harris asked.

He was not listening to me, but I continued.

'The ships that ply their trade between Ireland, England, France, and other destinations.'

'How interesting,' he replied, absentmindedly.

We walked along in silence and then an amazing thing happened.

'Jonathan, you are a genius!'

'A genius? What's brought this on?'

'The ships plying their trade; that's what this is all about. I've been a fool. How could I have not seen it? Come, Jonathan, we might still be in time.'

He rushed like a maniac from the beach towards the hotel with me in hot pursuit.

\*\*\*

We hurried past the guests in the foyer, who up till then had been snoozing in the armchairs, and then arrived at the reception desk. Once there, Harris extracted a hard-covered, black notebook from his inside pocket. He opened it and began turning the pages. The startled receptionist was looking at us in amazement. Eventually, he found what he was looking for and, turning to the receptionist, said, 'Would you connect me to this phone number please – Galway 274. It is most urgent.'

The efficient young lady acted with haste and soon I heard her say, 'I have an urgent call for you.' She handed the phone to Harris.

'Could I speak to Inspector Hennessy?' he asked.

I watched as Harris waited anxiously. I could not fathom what was going on. One minute we were strolling on the beach and, the next, Harris was making an urgent phone call to our friend, Inspector Hennessy.

'Hello Inspector; it's Harris.'

I could not hear all the conversation, as Harris had his back to me, but at one stage he said,

'The registration number of the van?' He turned towards me and stared right past me, the telephone in his hand. 'Just give a moment,' he said, 'it is here somewhere.' He continued to stare at nothing in particular and then calmly read out the full registration number of the van. 'It is dark green in colour, the tax disc is five months out of date and there is a small crack on the left-hand side of the windscreen.'

I had witnessed, once again, that photographic memory in action.

The conversation lasted for another few minutes, then, as he was finishing, he turned towards me and I heard him say, 'Thank you so much for your help; I felt that, by going directly to you, I could speed matters along. Will you phone me here when you have news?'

He returned the phone to its cradle, thanked the receptionist, and said, 'We will just have to wait until Inspector Hennessy phones back. It might be a long wait.'

'Why in heaven's name did you contact Hennessy?'

'To tell him to locate the van and have the crate, that is on the back of it, opened.'

'What crate?' Did we not see it smashed behind the caravan.'

'That was not the Christies crate-it is now on the back of the van with something in it.'

'Really?'

'Nelson, the notorious criminal, is in the crate.'

I was dumbfounded.

'Let's retire to the bar for a drink and I will explain everything.'

***

We sat down and, in a measured tone, Harris began his remarkable account of what was happening.

'The events of the past few days have centered entirely on getting a Christie's crate and putting Nelson inside it. Then the crate would be put aboard a ship and taken out of this country. It is an extraordinary story, and they might have succeeded were it not for your remark about a ship plying its trade. There is a logical pathway to all solutions and everything, by some means or other, is linked. Take our present predicament. We have a man in a white suit who, by chance, happened to stay in the hotel this week. He could have booked in somewhere else, or we could have come down here on a different week.

'We know little about him and yet he is a person of interest. His dress and appearance leave much to be desired, but such matters are really no business of ours. There is a curiosity about him that niggles. He is staying here on his own. Unusual; his attendance at the preliminary auction viewing surprised me and his strange behaviour when we caught him measuring that statue troubled me.

'Then the preposterous action of buying his own statue at the auction; why would one do that? His manner and demeanour were interesting and, added to that, we had the mysterious man hiding in the caravan. Who was hiding there? I concluded that the person in the caravan was the main protagonist in this business, and our friend in the white suit was a sort of lackey, or maybe even a minder.

'I believe that when Nelson made his escape from the Four Courts in Dublin, he was immediately driven to the caravan in Rosslare by our man in the white suit. It takes time to set up checkpoints and roadblocks and before they could be put in place, he was perhaps fifty miles or more down the road. The escape was meticulously planned by associates of Nelson. It is important to remember that the Christie's auction was advertised in the national newspapers and came to the attention of either Nelson or his associates. It was then that the plan was hatched to have Nelson transferred out of the country in the Christie's crate.

'I'm not fully sure but imagine I am correct in surmising that the statue of George Washington had, some days prior to the escape, been delivered and placed in or adjacent to the caravan at Rosslare. It would have been in a crate when it arrived at the caravan. It was removed from it and delivered to Ashford Manor. We saw it being carried in the front door. When the statue was eventually sold at the auction, it was placed in a Christie's crate and brought back to the caravan field. The statue was immediately taken from the crate and buried near the sand dunes. Nelson sat into the empty crate and it was sealed once more. The smashed crate we saw behind the caravan was the one that had arrived in Rosslare from Dublin a few days earlier.'

'I understand all this,' I said, 'but why was our devious friend measuring another statue that first morning at Ashford Manor?'

'I surmise that Nelson and his friends had seen a picture of the Greek god in the catalogue and realised its dimensions were close to that of the George

Washington statue. They told him to measure it and confirm that was the case. In the unlikely event of something untoward happening at the auction, which might prevent them from being successful in their bid for the George Washington statue, they could then bid for the Greek god and the day would be saved.'

'But were they not always going to have the winning bid at the auction for the George Washington statue?'

'Yes, but they were leaving nothing to chance. They had to get that crate from Christie's. That attitude and attention to detail shows how devious these criminals are. It was when you mentioned the ship plying its trade that the strange behavior of our old Etonian friend began to make sense. Jonathan, if you wished to smuggle someone out of the country, by ship, how would you go about it?'

Rhetorical; no response required.

'Some people would attempt the stowaway method and hide aboard a ship. Why not do the unorthodox, the unexpected thing and smuggle the person aboard under the noses of the Customs and Excise people? That is exactly what our friend in the white suit is attempting to do as we speak.'

'Really?'

'You recall when I purchased the figurine and went to collect it and settle my account?'

'Yes.'

'You must have noticed how it had been placed in a small timber box and wrapped in brown paper and tied with Christie's distinctive tape. I was even asked if I required clearance papers in case I was exporting it.'

'Yes, I remember that.'

'This is what the whole thing is about – getting a crate out of this country without it being examined by the customs authorities.'

'Surely they would request that the crate be opened for examination?'

'Cast your mind back to your days in Egypt. Remember when you were involved in the shipping of items of antiquity to England through Port Said? Would they not have been labelled in such a way that they were treated with care and passed through Customs and Excise expeditiously, without examination?'

'Yes, now that I think about it, I'm certain that is what happened.'

'Exactly. All the paperwork was prepared by professionals and the crates were properly labelled by the Antiquities Department of Egypt. In most circumstances, the Customs and Excise people at any port will inspect the contents of a crate before allowing it to be loaded onto a ship. But the crate I am referring to is emblazoned with the markings of Christie's of London, with a declaration attached that states the contents are that of a statue valued at £300. It would also state that it was a work of art and exempt from customs duty. You may be certain that, in such circumstances, the crate would be loaded without inspection.'

\*\*\*

It was much later that evening when a phone call from the Guards' station in Galway came through. Harris went out to the reception desk to take the call. He was gone for at least twenty minutes and I remained in the hotel bar, waiting for him. When he returned, it was obvious from the expression on his face that the news was good.

'Well, it's all over,' he said. 'Nelson has been apprehended and is, as I speak, on his way to Mountjoy Jail in Dublin.'

'Was there any trouble?'

'No. The lorry was stopped at a new roadblock, on the far side of Dublin, about five miles from the border with Northern Ireland.'

I did the calculations and said, 'That is amazing. They travelled almost one hundred and fifty miles without being stopped.'

'They were stopped alright, at two roadblocks which had been in place since Nelson's escape from the Four Courts, one on the way into Dublin City, the other on the far side of the road to Belfast. This all occurred prior to my phone call to Inspector Hennessy. The crate was examined each time but not opened. The Guards and soldiers manning the roadblock were impressed with the packaging and the Christie's name. The paperwork was in order and there was a Customs and Excise clearance certificate stapled to one side of the crate which stated that the contents consisted of a work of art; a statue. Our friend in the white suit informed the officer in charge that he was on his way to Belfast to catch the ship leaving for Liverpool later that evening.

'Following my phone call to the Inspector, he had the registration number and description of the van circulated to every roadblock. It was very quickly established that the van had just cleared the second one on the far side of Dublin. An additional roadblock was put in place as quickly as possible and the van was halted five miles short of the Irish border. The man in the white suit, a Mr Andrew Jackson, was arrested and taken into custody. An officer from the Guards got into the small lorry and drove it, under escort, to the nearest Guards' station. The crate was then unloaded and placed in a secure enclosure within the Guards' station grounds.

'Can you just imagine the expression on Nelson's face when the crate was opened and he saw the assembled small army pointing their guns and rifles at him. The game was up and he offered no resistance.'

'That clears that up,' I said,' but there's one thing that mystifies me.'

'Only one thing?' Harris remarked.

'Yes; this photographic memory of yours baffles me. I have seen you resort to it many times in the past. Your face sort of glazes over and you appear to go into some sort of trance. How were you able to conjure up the registration number of the van and the other details about it?

'It is this brain of mine. Everything I observe – and it is the same for everyone – is stored there, and can be recalled in an instant. In my case, there is a bit more going on. You and I saw the small lorry being unloaded outside the Ashford Manor a few days ago. In your mind, now, you can still see a picture of it, and would recognise the lorry if you saw it again, but you can detect very little else. As for me, I am looking at a photograph of the lorry as we speak. I can see every single detail of it. By enlarging the photograph stored in my brain, I can clearly see the registration number and numerous other details. Your brain, in common with that of most people, does not have that facility.

'Allow me to give you an example. When we entered this lounge a short while ago, I subconsciously looked at the display of bottles on the shelves of the bar. A photograph of that display is fixed in my brain but I will never have any use for it and, in time, it will almost disappear and just become a vague recollection.'

'But can you still see it now?'

'Yes, it is there, stored in my brain and I can call it up if I want to."

'Really? What if I were to test you? With that be offensive?"

'By no means, I would welcome such a challenge.'

'On the middle shelf of the bar, there is an object lodged between two bottles. Can you tell me what it is?'

He had his back to the bar and was looking directly at me. I saw that glazed look appear on his face as he stared beyond me for a few moments. Then he spoke.

'On the third shelf there it is a soft-backed red notebook wedged between a bottle of Hennessy brandy and a bottle of Powers whiskey. The notebook is almost new and in excellent condition. There is a black pencil lying beside the notebook. The whiskey bottle is full and the brandy bottle is almost empty.'

\*\*\*

The following morning, as we made our way back to Mannane, I was still marvelling at the impromptu memory display I had witnessed the evening before in the bar. I had been privileged to witness Harris' remarkable photographic memory in action but I knew he had only done it for me and that he would never do it again.

It was late afternoon when we approached the village of Ballinasloe. In a field on the left-hand side of the road a large sign had been erected. In bold letters, at least six feet high, it read, *COME TO GALWAY RACES*. I wasn't to know the significance of the large sign and the part we would play in that horse race meeting in two months' time. It was to be our next sensational adventure.

# ABOUT THE AUTHOR

Tony O'Connor lives on the east coast of Ireland in the seaside village of Blackrock Co. Louth with his wife Marie. He is a retired accountant, and began writing the stories 15 years ago. He has written twelve. The majority of the books are set in Connemara, Co. Galway Ireland

Printed in Great Britain
by Amazon